Maggie Conway spent the first ten years of her life in London before moving to Scotland. She has a degree in English Literature and spent many years dreaming of pursuing her passion for writing.

A perfect day would include an early morning swim, a good coffee, a great book and a few hours spent writing before the chaos of a husband, three children, a dog and a cat begins.

Having landed the role of chief dog walker, she spends far too much time roaming the streets but at least this gives her a chance to think up new storylines.

Winter at West Sands Guest House

Maggie Conway

ONE PLACE. MANY STORIES

HQ

An imprint of HarperCollins*Publishers* Ltd
1 London Bridge Street
London SE1 9GF

This paperback edition 2018

1

First published in Great Britain by
HQ, an imprint of HarperCollins*Publishers* Ltd 2017

ISBN: 9780008308612

MIX
Paper from
responsible sources
FSC™ C007454

This book is produced from independently certified FSC™ paper to ensure responsible forest management.

For more information visit: www.harpercollins.co.uk/green

Printed and bound in Great Britain by
CPI Group, Croydon CR0 4YY

Dedicated to John Conway, an extraordinary man.

Thank-you, Dad.

Chapter One

Eva Harris wasn't spying, not exactly. It was more a case of taking a healthy interest in her new neighbours. She'd almost jumped for joy when the removal van had pulled up earlier. During the afternoon she'd taken several breaks from her painting, lingering at the window with mugs of tea, hoping to catch a glimpse of whoever had moved in.

It must have been one of the most efficient removals ever – the van appeared to have come and gone in record time and apart from the removal men Eva hadn't seen anyone. Even now all was quiet, a sleek black car in the driveway the only evidence anyone had moved in.

Eva hated not having neighbours. She found the silence from next door unsettling. The house – known affectionately as Mac's place – had lain empty, ever since Moira and Donald MacKenzie had decided to sell up and cruise around the world before moving into a bungalow to accommodate Donald's arthritis. Tempted as she was to rush round to welcome her new neighbours, she held off. She knew moving day could be hectic and it was probably better to give whoever it was time to settle in.

From where she stood at a bedroom window on her first floor, Eva looked out onto the harbour and beyond that to the expanse of sea. Even now in October, St Andrews was a beautiful place to live. Being close to the university, Eva was used to seeing students coming and going along the cobbled streets. Tonight though, everyone was huddled up against the rain, hurrying to wherever they had to go.

Turning from the window, Eva rested her hands on her hips and admired the silky finish of the duck egg blue wall she had just painted. Listening to the radio as the rain lashed against the window, she'd been happy to be indoors today and even happier that she had managed to paint the whole room despite all her neighbour-spotting activity.

Eva loved running her small guest house and even though visitors came to St Andrews all year round, she closed during the winter months. This gave her time to take care of any maintenance and freshen up the rooms. But more importantly it gave her time to be with her son Jamie and it let them have the house to themselves without guests.

Looking at the time she realized he should be home by now, even allowing for his football after school. She pulled her phone from the back pocket of her dungarees but there were no messages from him. She resisted the urge to phone and check where he was.

Eva was convinced when she gave birth to Jamie a worry bead had been planted in her brain at the same time. Whatever the stage – teething, feeding, learning to read or to cross the road safely – Eva was always capable of imagining the worst-case scenario and only her constant vigilance prevented disaster. Each milestone brought its joys of course but also a new set of anxieties for Eva. Jamie was almost twelve now; the teenage years were looming large and the thought terrified her.

Starting high school had been a big change not just for Jamie but Eva too. With his new routine and all the after-school activities, she knew she had to give him a bit of independence but she'd been holding the reins of motherhood so tightly for so long it was difficult to let go. She wondered if she should phone Heather to see if she'd heard from Fraser. She could bet wherever Fraser was, Jamie would be two steps away.

When Jamie had come home after his first day at primary school and announced he had a new best friend called Fraser, Eva was more than relieved to meet his mum, Heather. Like their sons, their friendship had been instant and enduring. When Eva had admitted to her excessive – bordering neurotic – worrying, Heather had taken it in her stride. To this day Eva had never seen her friend stressed despite having three boisterous sons.

Heather had seen most things at least once and over the years Eva had called upon her expertise several times. When Jamie got his finger stuck in a bottle, kept bringing home bugs, or had decided jumping off furniture was fun, Heather reassured her that was what boys did. The only thing Heather hadn't managed to bestow on Eva was the ability to relax, at least not without alcohol being involved. Eva loved spending time at her friend's chaotic home but never knew if it was because of the easy atmosphere or because of her friend's willingness to produce a bottle of wine at any time for any reason.

No, she wouldn't phone Heather. She'd only remind her – again – they were lucky living in a small safe community, they'd agreed the boys were old enough to walk home from high school themselves, and they'd be home soon.

Swallowing the familiar tug of anxiety in her stomach, Eva took a deep breath and started tidying up. She placed the lid back on the paint pot, put the brushes in a jar of water, and went over in her head what she still had to do. Tomorrow she could start to put the furniture back in place and then give everything a good clean.

Eva was using a small ceramic seahorse sculpture as her inspiration to give the room a coastal feel. A couple of patterned navy cushions for the armchair and a beautiful driftwood mirror she'd found in a craft shop would provide the finishing touches.

She'd certainly come a long way in the seven years since she'd taken over West Sands guest house. When she'd moved in, the existing rooms were functional but drab. At school the only subject Eva had ever really enjoyed was art and she had discovered a real passion for interiors and decorating. Realizing she had a choice to either pay someone to do the work or learn how to do it herself, she chose the latter.

She'd enrolled in a painting and decorating course at a local college for one day a week that fitted in with Jamie's school hours and after that she'd kept going, learning with books, online courses, and a lot of trial and error. Now she was able to tackle most jobs herself and loved it so much – dreaming up colour combinations or imagining how textures might work in a room and then putting all her ideas into practice – she sometimes thought she'd missed her calling.

She liked to give each room an individual feel but it was also important to keep things fairly neutral and, above all, comfortable. The other two guest rooms wouldn't be decorated this year, just a thorough clean and a check everything was in working order. She folded the stepladders, propped them against the wall, and clicked off the radio just in time to hear the front door bang shut.

'Mum?' Eva felt herself relax at the sound of her son's voice.

'Up here! I'll be down in a sec.' Wiping her hands on her dungarees Eva headed downstairs, almost being knocked down by Hamish as he hurtled down after her. The reality of having a (literally barking mad) dog was proving to be very different from the one Eva imagined when she had finally given in to Jamie's constant pleading. Eva could think of a hundred reasons why not to get a dog but Jamie's single reason – he wanted a dog because he didn't have a brother or sister – trumped hers. Really, how could she refuse?

Dogs and guests weren't necessarily an ideal mix but Eva, always on the lookout for new target markets, had an idea and one she hoped would be a sound business move. Her master plan was to become a dog-friendly guest house. With its beautiful beaches and coastal paths, St Andrews was the ideal destination for dog lovers and she could tap into that. She'd have to look into it properly before the start of next season, find out about any legal requirements and change her website and marketing so guests would know she welcomed dogs.

'You'll have to train the dog properly and it won't be allowed in the kitchen,' she'd said to Jamie for the hundredth time as they had driven to the rescue centre.

'I promise, Mum,' he had replied solemnly. Jamie had fallen in love on sight with the mournful eyes of a scruffy brown and white crossbreed staring at him through the bars of a cage. Eva liked that he was small and – according to the lovely lady at the rescue centre – would be easy to train. That had been four weeks ago and so far, easy wasn't a word Eva would use.

In the hall, Eva ignored the trail of bags, jumpers, and football boots for now. Her eleven-year-old son's tendency to go into a strop didn't need any encouragement the minute he walked through the door. She found Jamie in the living room, his blond hair askew and long gangly limbs sprawled on the sofa with Hamish darting about ecstatically to welcome him home. Although Jamie shared Eva's fair colouring, at times he looked so like Paul it broke her heart and all Eva wanted was to wrap her arms around him the way she had always done. But eleven was an awkward age. Sometimes still her little boy who needed reassurance but also an aspiring adult who didn't always welcome hugs from his mum.

'Hi, sweetheart. How was school?' Eva asked him.

'Fine,' he replied using his standard response to most questions these days as he ruffled Hamish's ears. The days of waiting at the primary school gates with other parents, swapping and verifying information before walking home while Jamie chatted non-stop already felt like a distant memory to Eva. It was early days, she reminded herself. There was so much for him to take in and he was bound to communicate more when he was ready. Overcome with excitement, Hamish suddenly leapt onto the sofa beside Jamie.

'Off the sofa, Hamish!' Eva yelled.

'Mu-um! That's not the right voice remember? You're supposed to use a firm but calm voice,' Jamie said, mimicking Mrs Duffy from puppy training class.

Eva grimaced apologetically. 'You're right, I'm sorry.'

Jamie rolled off the sofa, giggling with delight as Hamish jumped on top of him and began slobbering all over his face. 'Hamish – yeuch!' he cried.

Eva grinned at them, relishing the moments when getting a dog did actually make sense.

'So, did you have a good game of football?' Eva asked.

'Nah, our team lost.' Jamie sniffed.

Sports mad like his father had been – Eva always felt a disappointment for not getting excited about penalty shoot-outs or understanding offside. She'd coped with the dinosaur stage, learning the difference between a T. rex and a stegosaurus. She'd actually enjoyed mastering the techniques to build bridges and cars from Lego and she even knew every character from *Star Wars*. But she had never managed to grasp the intricacies of The Beautiful Game. Of course if Paul was here, they could talk football father to son, the way it should be.

'I expected you home before now.' Eva tried to keep her voice neutral.

'It's no big deal, Mum – we were just chatting a bit after the game,' Jamie retorted, wiping an arm across his dirt-streaked face.

'I don't have a problem with that. But how about a text next time? Just to let me know if you're going to be later. We agreed if you got a mobile phone you would keep in touch.' Eva wondered how many times she had given the 'keep in touch' speech. Even she was fed up with the sound of her own voice saying the same thing over and over.

Their wrestling match now over, Jamie got up from the floor while Hamish, tired out by his exertions, flopped dramatically on the floor.

'Mum?' Jamie came and stood beside Eva, almost the same height as her now, his blue eyes fixing her with a challenging stare. 'Have you thought about it yet?'

Eva's heart sank. 'Er, not properly yet.'

'I need to let them know by next week. All my friends are going; I'll be the only one not going,' he pleaded, his face settling into a petulant pout.

'I know that, but –'

'Then why can't I go?' he demanded.

'Let me think about it and I promise we'll talk later, okay?' She knew she was stalling. But how could she just say yes to a trip that meant her son would be hurling himself off cliffs, diving into water and God knows what else. The weekend trip, organized by his football club, might promise to be a great team-bonding adventure but the very thought of it made Eva come out in a cold sweat.

And she wasn't sure how she would cope with him being away. Apart from the odd sleepover she'd never been separated from him. Eva could almost hear Paul's voice telling her not to worry, just to relax and let him go. But he wasn't here now and it was all down to her.

Eva plumped up a pillow, switching to a safer topic. 'Are you hungry?' Jamie's face broke into the cheeky grin she knew so well and Eva felt her heart melt. 'Why don't you pick up your things in the hall and go for a shower and I'll get something ready to eat.'

'Okay.' He slouched off but stopped and turned at the door. 'I meant to say – I saw a light on in Mac's place when I was coming home.'

Eva nodded. 'There was a removal van there earlier today. The new people have moved in.'

'Who will it be?'

Eva smiled at how young he could suddenly sound, as if she would always have the answers. 'I don't know. But I guess we'd better stop calling it Mac's place.'

Eva heard Jamie and Hamish thundering up the stairs as she went into the kitchen to heat the lasagne she had made earlier. Switching on the oven, she wondered how her new neighbours were and hoped everything was going well for whoever it was. After all, she knew how difficult moving day could be.

***

A cold January day, it had snowed the day Eva and Jamie moved in to West Sands guest house. It had been the day her confidence had suddenly crumbled and she questioned whether she could really do this. As she unlocked the door to their new home, Jamie was sobbing miserably with a streaming cold and Eva could have quite easily dissolved into a pool of tears herself. Suddenly it all seemed such a grown-up thing to do, move into a big house and be responsible for it all, not something a twenty-six-year-old widow with a young child could do.

After her husband Paul had died, everyone seemed to have an opinion as to what Eva should now do with her life, not least her mother. Although she had been visibly upset at Paul's funeral – he was impossible not to like – Eva had sensed a quiet sense of satisfaction from her that it had all gone wrong just as she'd predicted.

She had wasted no time in seizing her chance. 'Come home, darling. Let me look after you.' Which in Helen Devine's language translated to 'let me take over your life again'. The way she had when Eva lived at home. Sometimes it had felt as if her mother had controlled Eva's whole life. Suggesting suitable friends, the right clothes to wear, or where to go on holiday.

From the depths of her despair Eva managed to look up just enough to see her mother's clutches coming towards her and knew she had to act quickly. Her priority was finding somewhere she and Jamie could feel safe and rebuild their lives together. But she also had to think of a way of supporting them in the future.

Randomly searching the internet for property, she stumbled on one for sale in St Andrews already being run as a guest house. Eva remembered one of her favourite childhood games of playing hotels and felt something stir within her. Could she turn that fantasy from all those years ago into a reality? A business that would let her be self-sufficient and be there for her young son – it sounded perfect.

The money from Paul's life insurance meant she was able to put in an offer and when it was accepted, Eva was elated and horrified all at the same time. Helen's reaction to her daughter's idea had been less idealistic. 'Do you like plunging toilets and cleaning carpet stains?' she had asked. With her mother's caustic words ringing in her head, Eva stood in the hall that first day trying to comfort Jamie, terrified she had made a huge mistake. Overwhelmed and exhausted, Eva had a sudden desire to crawl into a warm bed and sleep for a week.

And then out of that dark moment, Moira MacKenzie appeared at the door like a beacon of light, bringing hope – and a pot of home-made soup – to Eva. Wearing layers of bright clothes, her copper-red hair piled haphazardly on top of her head and bangles jangling at her wrists, something about her presence immediately put Eva at ease.

She'd felt guilty for doing it, but it was impossible not to compare Moira to her own mother. Of course Eva knew her mother loved her. But it was a neatly wrapped kind of love that came with air kisses. She wasn't the type of woman who made you want to lose yourself in a big-bosomed hug the way Moira MacKenzie did.

Moira and her husband Donald were both retired academics and ran a second-hand bookshop in St Andrews. The two women chatted comfortably as Moira helped Eva to unpack and settle Jamie into his new room. Eva wasn't sure if they would have made it through those first few days without her and had counted her lucky stars a thousand times over the years that the MacKenzies were her neighbours. Kind, caring, and just a tiny bit eccentric. Eva loved them. Although their own children had grown and left, their house was always full of grandchildren and friends coming and going.

Eva's heart sank the day Moira told her the house had been sold. A few weeks later Eva tearfully waved them off, happy for them but secretly wishing things didn't have to change. The house had lain empty for a few weeks and it had been difficult to see it sitting silently. It was only then Eva realized just how much she had depended on the MacKenzies' presence next door. How since they had left, a sense of loneliness seemed to have engulfed her.

***

What kind of an idiot buys a house without seeing it first? An idiot like me, thought Ben Matthews knocking back a couple of painkillers with a mouthful of coffee. Leaning against the window he looked out at the view from his new front living room. In the distance he could see the swell of the dark sea. He ran his hand through his hair, realizing this was going to take some getting used to. The world felt quiet here, so different from the constant noise and buzz of the city.

He had left London ridiculously early this morning. The journey had been long and hard; only the thought of the removal van a couple of hours behind had spurred him on. He had finally arrived in St Andrews in the early afternoon and headed straight to the solicitor's office where he'd dealt with a barrage of legal documentation and polite questions as quickly as possible. Armed with keys and directions to his new home he drove through the town, only stopping to grab a few groceries. From what he could see, the cobbled streets and historic architecture looked charming and quaint and, more importantly, as different from London as he had hoped.

He found the house easily enough: the last property in a row of impressive Victorian houses facing the beach. He'd climbed out of the car, rolling the tension out of his shoulders as he took in his new surroundings. The house itself sat well back from the road, the front lawn flanked by a gravelled driveway on one side and overgrown flowerbeds on the other.

He glanced over at the neighbouring house – similar to his except for the ivy cascading down the soft red brick of its front wall and spilling over a blue front door. To the other side of the house there was nothing to see except the sweep of sand and sea stretching into the distance. After unloading the car, he'd let himself in, dumped his suitcases in the hall, and waited for the delivery van.

By anyone's standards it must seem mad that the day he moved into his new house was the first time he'd actually stepped into it. But he had left it all to Samantha. It had been she who had flown up to Scotland to view the house while Ben stayed to close his last big deal.

Telling Samantha he wanted to leave London and return to teaching, he hadn't been sure how she would react. She was a city girl through and through but she seemed to go for it, shared his vision for a new life. She appeared genuinely excited by Ben's job offer at the University of St Andrews, providing the obligatory bottle of something expensive to celebrate.

Ben thought they might rent somewhere first but Samantha had insisted on viewing an amazing house she'd seen online located right on the beachfront. Houses weren't really his thing but Ben had happily looked at the photos and listened to her plans for the house, including turning one of the rooms into her office where she planned to set up and run an IT consultancy.

Turning from the window he shook his head and smiled wryly to himself. She had been right of course. It was a beautiful house, an estate agent's dream to sell with its original fireplaces, cornice ceilings, and large bay windows overlooking the sea. A stunning house but clearly not enough for Samantha. Not enough for her to be able to decline the promotion offered to her by the company she worked for just weeks before they were set to move. Their expansion into East Asia provided her with an opportunity simply 'too good to turn down'.

Ben wondered if she'd just got cold feet about them, about the whole move. She didn't ask him to stay and he hadn't offered to. Money wasn't an issue and the sale of the house was in his name anyway so all he had to do was come alone. A strange almost unspoken ending of whatever it was they had. What did that say about their relationship?

He took the last mouthful of the coffee, thankful he'd had the sense to mark a box with kitchen stuff so at least he had been able to find the kettle and cups. Apart from that, he didn't know where anything was and wasn't sure he'd have the energy to unpack anything tonight, let alone try and find the bedding. His stomach suddenly rumbled in protest at the measly sandwich he'd eaten earlier on the motorway and a sudden chill crept over him. It was all meant to be so different. To think he'd actually imagined the possibility of a family one day, but now the empty rooms only served to remind him how alone he was.

He walked into the large hall where most of the boxes sat untouched. He hadn't brought much. He'd made a decision only to bring what was important and there had been surprisingly little to pack. His books, some photos, and a few essential pieces of furniture. He had left London after all those years and realized he didn't have much to bring at all.

***

Eva decided she couldn't wait. She simply had to go and meet her new neighbours and felt a flutter of anticipation as she slipped on her jacket and ventured out into the wet night. Earlier she'd driven Jamie and his friend Ewan to Scouts and Jamie would be dropped home later. Leaving her own front door, it took Eva only seconds to walk down the front path of her own house and up her neighbour's.

She remembered all the times she'd walk straight round to the back, knock on the door, and just walk in. Eva would immediately be enveloped by the warmth of the kitchen and Moira would have the kettle on before Eva had time to sit down at the massive oak table, which was always strewn with books and papers.

Reaching the little porch Eva shook the rain from her hood, noticing the fine layer of dust on the little shelf where a potted plant used to sit. Through the opaque glass of the inner door she could see a light on in the hall. She knocked on the familiar door feeling a little bubble of excitement in her chest, thinking how lovely it would be to have neighbours again.

After a few moments the door opened and whoever Eva might have imagined opening the door, she wasn't prepared for the man who now did. Tall, wearing a black T-shirt and blue jeans, his dark hair was tousled, as if he'd just run a hand through it. But it was the intensity of the dark brown eyes looking at her questioningly that struck Eva and made her instantly feel self-conscious and awkward. His features were handsome but the deep frown etched into them made Eva feel uneasy.

She cleared her throat and smiled brightly at him. 'Hi. I'm Eva Harris. I live next door with my son and wanted to come and welcome you.'

He regarded her for a moment before holding out his hand and introducing himself. 'Ben Matthews. Nice to meet you.'

They shook hands, his touch sending a small shockwave through Eva. Suddenly she wasn't sure what to do. The scenario she had played out in her head of this meeting hadn't included her standing like a speechless idiot. Granted, that was before she knew her new neighbour looked like ... well, like this. But that was no reason to behave differently; she was simply here to welcome him and in keeping with the tradition set by Mrs MacKenzie, she held out a pot of her best broth.

'I brought you some soup.'

He glanced down at it, looking slightly baffled. And certainly not as grateful as Eva had hoped for.

'That's kind of you, but you didn't have to do that.'

She shook her head. 'It's no problem. I know moving day can be difficult and you might not have had time to think about food. It's home-made, vegetable ...' Her voice trailed off and she swallowed nervously.

'Thank you.' He took the pot from her hands and placed it awkwardly on a pile of boxes behind him.

'I know lots of people are vegetarian these days so I thought that would be the safest option.' Eva heard herself babble on, wishing she could stop but sure that if she did there would be a horrible silence. Deciding she had exhausted the soup topic, she changed tack. 'So, have you come far today?'

'London.'

She nodded. 'St Andrews is going to be quite a change for you then.'

'That's the general idea,' he said dryly.

Eva couldn't understand why he was making this so difficult and thought desperately of what to say next. She never had a problem talking to new people; she did it all the time with her guests. She had been thinking along the lines of a cosy get-to-know-you chat, possibly over a cup of tea, while she imparted

17

her local knowledge and offered to help with anything. Well she could at least still do that.

'So, um, is there anything I can help you with?'

'Unless you're a heating engineer I doubt it,' he replied, not even bothering to hide his irritability. Now that she thought about it, there had been no surge of warmth when he had opened the door. In fact she could sense a definite chill coming from the house.

'You don't have heating?' No wonder he was scowling. These were big houses to heat and to arrive after a long journey to find no heating would test anyone.

'Have you checked the pressure gauge?'

His brows shot up. 'Sorry?'

'Well no, I'm not a heating engineer but I'd guess the water pressure to the boiler might have dropped because it hasn't been used for a while. You need to refill your system by opening the bypass valve.'

Not waiting for an invitation, she walked in past him just happy she was able to help. A wall of cold air hit Eva as she entered the house and she shivered. She recalled all the times she had been here to see the MacKenzies, the house always so warm and inviting. But it was more than the cold. There was something missing but Eva couldn't put her finger on it. A few boxes here and there but otherwise it all seemed too orderly, not enough chaos for someone who had just moved in.

She could see he had got as far as opening the door to the small hall cupboard where the boiler was located. Using her phone torch Eva squeezed into the cupboard and knelt down. Below the boiler she found the bypass valve and opened it for a few seconds before hearing the satisfying sound of the boiler ignite.

'That's it. You should start to feel a difference soon.' Straightening up she found herself face to face with him. Or face to chest actually – he really was tall. She tucked a strand of hair behind her ear, his nearness making her conscious she hadn't given her appearance a moment's thought before she came round. She raised her gaze to meet his and thought she detected the tiniest flicker of amusement in his eyes.

'So is fixing boilers a hobby of yours?' he asked.

'I run a guest house next door. I've had to learn to deal with leaky taps, blocked sinks –'

'Guest house?' The frown made another appearance. As a businesswoman, Eva knew it was vital to be on good terms with her neighbours and was keen to reassure him.

'Please don't be alarmed. I only open May to September. All my guests are highly respectable, usually out all day, and tucked up nice and early so you'll hardly know they're here. They won't disturb you.'

Appearing reassured with this information he gave a small, forced smile. 'Well, thank you. It was beginning to feel pretty miserable in here.'

'These properties don't take care of themselves. I can give you the name of a local heating engineer if you like – probably best to give the system an overhaul.'

'Um, sure,' he muttered.

'So what brings you to St Andrews?' Eva asked following him back through the hall towards the front door.

'I'm starting work at the university.'

Eva nodded, not surprised. Lots of people coming to St Andrews had some connection to the university. In the summer much of her business came from families attending graduations and Eva was happy to play a small part in these special occasions.

'It's a good university and has a great reputation. My friend's son has just started studying engineering there,' she spoke chattily. 'So, um, what will you be doing there?'

He ran a hand over his shadowed jaw, hesitated for a moment as if reluctant to divulge any information. 'Teaching physics,' he replied simply.

Eva had no idea what the average physicist looked like these days but was surprised. Certainly there was a serious, almost brooding quality about him but for some reason teaching physics seemed at odds with his appearance. But perhaps it explained his reticence. Maybe he was one of those genius types who found it difficult to communicate with people unless they had some super high IQ.

Eva closed her mouth, which she realized was hanging open, and gave herself a shake. 'Well, I'm sure you'll enjoy living in St Andrews. It's a friendly community and being at the university you'll soon meet lots of people.' Although Eva got the impression Ben Matthews wasn't going to be actively seeking new friends.

Meeting visitors from all over the world, Eva reckoned she had become a pretty good judge of character. Some wanted to chat; others preferred keeping to themselves. She knew some people were easy to please while others found fault in everything. And now she sensed Ben Matthews was being guarded.

For someone who had just moved in, the place didn't show many signs of a life on the move. Everything pointed to him being on his own, which seemed strange for such a big house. She mulled that over in her head: the fact he appeared to be single. Did it matter to her? If she was honest she'd been hoping a family might move in, maybe with children close to Jamie's age. Perhaps he had a wife, a partner or family still to join him.

'Once you get settled perhaps you and er ... well perhaps you'd like to come round for dinner?'

He had reached the front door now, placed his hand on the handle, and she saw him bristle. 'I doubt I'll have time. I'm going to be pretty busy.'

'So, um is it just you? I mean, there's no one else?' She cringed inwardly at how nosy she just sounded but couldn't help herself.

'No, it's just me,' he replied tersely, opening the door.

'Right, of course,' Eva said weakly, stepping outside. She suddenly remembered something and turned. 'I still have a set of keys for this house. The people who lived here before you – we had a set of each other's keys for emergencies.' If she hoped he might say to keep the arrangement in place – after all it was a sensible neighbourly thing to do – then she was to be disappointed.

'Just put them through the letterbox next time you're passing.' His tone suggested he was finding this conversation tedious now, making Eva feel as if she was being dismissed.

'Of course.'

'Thanks again,' he said closing the front door behind her. Eva hurried back to her own house with the rain still falling, feeling suddenly miserable. What had she been thinking? That she could turn up and be welcomed with open arms? She was trying to be friendly but now had a horrible feeling he would just think her pushy and prying. Stupidly she thought she could re-create what she had with the MacKenzies. But of course, he was a stranger. And not a particularly friendly one by the looks of it.

Chapter Two

Ben hadn't worn a suit since his last day working in the city and wasn't enjoying wearing one now. It reminded him too much of the life he wanted to forget. Sometimes he wondered how he had endured it for five years. A job he hated but that earned him a shedload of money, a luxury apartment overlooking the Thames that he was hardly ever in, and people he socialized with but wouldn't count as real friends.

He'd got used to the crazy long hours, the cut and thrust of making deals. But during that time he'd never lost his passion for physics, the subject he'd studied at university. The only difference was that instead of using his mathematical skills to figure out how the universe began, he'd used them to predict how markets might react and make huge amounts of money. Well, he wasn't living the nightmare any more – today was a new beginning.

He fiddled with his shirt collar, feeling surprisingly nervous. He knew working at the university wouldn't normally require him to wear a suit but he wanted to make a good impression today. A good night's sleep would have helped but finding the bedding had proved too much and he'd finally given in to exhaustion and fallen asleep on the sofa. After only a few hours' sleep he had woken early this morning, his bones aching and his mind racing.

Of course the visit from his new neighbour hadn't exactly helped. Images of her had kept flitting into his head as he tried to fall asleep. He might be dog-tired and sworn off women for life but he still recognized a beautiful woman when he saw one. With her honey-blonde hair pulled into a ponytail, not a scrap of make-up – unless you counted what looked like a smudge of blue paint on her face – she was stunning.

But this was definitely not the time to start noticing the colour of your neighbour's hair. She'd just been so *friendly*, acting all neighbourly, but he hadn't been in the mood for twenty questions and to be honest, he hadn't known quite how to handle it. He knew he lived in a small community now and that's probably what neighbours did – talk to each other, borrow things – or in her case fix heating systems.

Their conversation last night was longer than any he'd had with his old neighbours in London. He'd never known their stories and hadn't wanted to; a nod in the hallway had sufficed. But he got the uncomfortable feeling it was going to be different with Eva Harris.

Was it just two of them living there? He'd noticed her hands were bare of rings and she'd only mentioned living with her son. If she was on her own running a business and bringing up a son, she'd have her hands full yet she had made time to bring him home-made soup. He'd found the gesture curiously quaint and he was well aware he hadn't exactly been gracious accepting it but it hadn't stopped him devouring the lot. It had tasted delicious.

He didn't know why her visit had irked him so much but he'd felt wrong-footed in some way, her questions reinforcing his isolation. Having to say out loud that he was on his own felt like admitting his dream lay in tatters and that had hurt more than he cared to admit and had been enough to drive his manners away. Next time he saw her he would make a point of thanking her but that didn't mean he wanted to get involved.

Giving himself a mental shake, he checked his tie in the mirror and headed downstairs. Today the house felt even bigger, his footsteps echoing on the polished wooden floorboards in the hall. He had no doubt it had been a well-loved and lived-in house, but it was crying out for some attention and updating. At least the shower had worked this morning even though it was rickety and had made a slightly alarming noise.

Wandering through to the dining room at the back of the house he could see the potential to make it a beautiful home if you knew how to go about it. He wouldn't have a clue where to start. Clearly it was too big for him. He'd be rattling about here on his own. A door led him through to the kitchen. Most people would want this as one big space, he imagined as he walked over to the large window overlooking the garden.

'What the – ?'

In dungarees on her knees at the bottom of his garden was his new neighbour, Eva Harris. She appeared to be chasing a chicken around his back garden. Other chickens were clucking around in her own garden and a small manic dog seemed to be getting in on the action also. Watching for a few moments Ben realized she seemed to be coaxing the chicken from his garden back into her own.

Unlike last night, her hair was loose, tumbling down her back in soft waves. He watched as she made a sudden lunge for the chicken and then hoisted it over the fence back into her own garden. Ben couldn't help smiling. God, she looked mad. And utterly beautiful. He shook his head and forced himself away from events in the garden, as enticing as they were.

Ben started to get some papers ready for his meeting. Walking back through the hall, an envelope caught his eye lying on the mat by the front door. Opening it, he found a set of keys. Clearly Eva Harris was an early riser and had returned the keys to his house. He tossed them onto the sideboard, ignoring the inexplicable stab of guilt he felt, and went to get ready.

***

'Come on, Betsy … this way!' Eva used her best chicken voice but Betsy was choosing to ignore her and instead seemed intent on pecking something interesting on the ground. There were times when Eva questioned her decision to rescue six chickens especially when it came to the weekly cleanout and even more so when they decided to go on walkabouts into other people's gardens.

She should have fixed that gap in the fence ages ago and hadn't noticed it had got big enough for an escape party. She loved her girls and it was wonderful being able to provide her guests with fresh eggs. But there was no doubt it had been a labour of love and it had been hard work to get them from the sad-looking creatures they once were to the cheeky happy characters they were now.

Spotting her moment, she grabbed Betsy with two hands and lifted her back to the safety of her own garden. Hamish, happy to have Betsy home safely, barked in approval. Eva had very carefully introduced Hamish and the chickens but she needn't have worried. They were all firm friends now and Eva suspected Hamish had assumed the role of pack leader.

Finding a piece of wood from her shed she dragged it over and managed to prop it up against the gap in the fence, hoping that would secure it until she could fix it properly. She doubted her new neighbour would appreciate a chicken on the loose in his garden; he was more likely to be the type to slab everything over with concrete.

Disappointment had given way to anger when she thought about him now. Eva began vigorously brushing up the dirty pine shavings from the coop, thinking just how rude he had been. She tossed the shavings onto the compost heap at the bottom corner of the garden and with some help from Hamish, rounded up the chickens. Ushering them back into their clean coop Eva left them to settle down and roost in peace.

Early morning was Eva's favourite time of day and getting up early to deal with guests had never been an issue. She loved being outside in her garden, and was making the most of it before the clocks went back and she would lose light in the morning. She trudged down to the bottom of the garden where she kept a small vegetable patch, enjoying the feel of muddy earth under her feet. It had been hit and miss with the success of her vegetable growing and her latest offering of carrots – slightly shrivelled and sorry-looking – had done nothing to convince Jamie eating vegetables could be a pleasurable experience.

Still, she loved that she had created a little safe haven for the two of them. Sometimes she wished she could lock the outside world out and just keep things the way they were. Ben Matthews's arrival had rankled her. Almost as if she blamed him – unfairly she knew – for making the MacKenzies leave and change everything.

A light rain was now falling and Eva started to feel chilled so she headed back towards the house with Hamish at her heels. She went in through the back door to the utility room, which had become a dumping ground for shoes, jackets, tools and old toys. Eva had cleared way to make room for Hamish's feeding bowls and basket, hoping she could train him to stay in this area and out of the kitchen.

'Hamish, here boy.' She pointed to his basket and was delighted when he obediently flopped into it. She gave him a treat and patted his head, thinking just maybe she was getting the hang of this training lark. She pulled off her wellies, slipped out of her dungarees, and washed up before heading upstairs.

In his darkened room Jamie slept soundly. She picked up a few random items of clothing and a *Harry Potter* book discarded on the floor by the side of his bed. Eva took a moment to watch him sleep, marvelling at the innocence of his sleeping young face. The smallest of smiles played on his lips as if he was in the middle of a lovely dream and Eva felt guilty for waking him.

She wished she had some sort of parental magic wand she could wave over him to keep him safe. He had been just four the day she'd woken him to go to the hospital after Paul's accident and Eva couldn't bear that she was about to wake him and bring tragedy into his life. Of course he wouldn't fully understand but somehow she was going to have to try and explain he would never see Daddy again. She could only hope the love and stability she provided would make up for his loss. Eva had always made sure Jamie knew who Paul was, sharing memories of him so her son knew he'd had a father who loved him very much.

Eva began the ritual of waking him, clicking on the bedside light and opening the curtains just enough to allow a sliver of grey morning light in through the gap. Jamie, not sharing his mother's love of mornings, rolled over in protest at the sudden intrusion into his slumber. 'Morning, love,' she said, giving him a gentle shake. Once she knew he was fully awake and in no danger of falling back to sleep, Eva left him to get dressed.

Returning to the kitchen with hot coffee on her mind, Eva felt the distinct crunch of cereal under her feet. Not necessarily an unusual occurrence but when she followed the trail of crumbs she found Hamish in his basket with his nose buried deep in a box of cereal. Clearly he had jumped up and taken it from the table, probably violating at least half a dozen health and safety regulations, thought Eva grimly.

'Oh, Hamish!' She snatched the box away and he looked up at her with guilty eyes. 'What am I going to do with you?' she sighed. Hamish, seeming to understand Eva's annoyance, crouched low in his basket, ears flattened against his head.

Eva tidied up and made herself a now much-needed coffee. She sat at the table with her hands wrapped around her mug, thinking of the day ahead. She glanced at the pile of papers and envelopes stacked on top of her laptop sitting in front of her on the table. The guest house always generated paperwork but she wasn't sure she was in the mood to face insurance quotes or marketing matters.

She'd do more work on the guest bedroom today. After several encouraging calls to Jamie he finally emerged from upstairs. Eva smiled to herself at his sudden interest in his appearance. Hair gel, spot cream, and a particular brand of deodorant had recently been added to Eva's weekly shopping list. Now his hair was neatly gelled into place and his school tie adjusted to what Eva presumed was an acceptably cool angle.

Donald MacKenzie had often stepped in to help Jamie master certain skills, including doing up his tie. His youngest grandson was a couple of years older than Jamie and Donald had always made a point of including Jamie when they did things together.

'Don't you look smart.' Eva smiled. He grunted as he plonked himself down at the table, tipping a huge amount of cereal into a bowl and splashing milk on the top. Eva started to spread butter on slices of bread and cut cheese for Jamie's lunch, going through her morning checklist.

'Have you packed your homework?' They'd spent a torturous hour last night doing his homework. Biology and then maths.

'In my bag.' He smiled sweetly before cramming a spoonful of cereal into his mouth.

'And you've got your PE kit?' Although Eva knew there wasn't much chance of him forgetting that.

'Yeah. And Mark's mum said it be okay for me and Fraser to go back to his house for a bit after badminton today.'

Eva racked her brain trying to remember if he had mentioned Mark before. 'Where does he live?'

'I dunno. It's near the school though.'

'Can you text me his address when you get there?'

'Yeah, all right.'

Eva was pleased he was making new friends but had to know all the details – the who, where, and when – before she could begin to feel anywhere near comfortable.

'So what time will you be home?'

He shrugged. 'Just like whenever.'

'I'll want you home for dinner though, okay?'

'Probably,' he sighed, clearly overwhelmed by the relentless questioning.

'I can come and collect you from Mark's house. Just text me but don't make it too late please,' Eva said, squashing the sandwich with an apple and yogurt into his lunchbox. He nodded taking his empty bowl over to the sink.

'You go and brush your teeth and I'll get Hamish ready for his walk.'

Going over to Hamish's basket, Eva stroked his velvety ears realizing just how grateful she was to have his company these days. She thought of the hours stretching ahead of her. Winter days could be long on her own and she was glad she had the bedroom to finish today.

She turned to Hamish, the cereal incident now forgotten. 'Come on, boy, it's you and me again. Time for your walk.' Hearing the magic word, Hamish jumped out of his basket and barked excitedly. Eva insisted on leaving the house together even though Jamie went to meet his friends to walk to school while she took Hamish in the opposite direction to the beach. When they were all ready to leave, Eva opened the front door, relieved to see it had stopped raining.

As if they had synchronized it, Eva heard her new neighbour's front door shut at the exact moment she closed her own and, glancing over, she saw Ben Matthews leave his house. She turned to Jamie and spoke between gritted teeth.

'Come on, we don't want to be late.' If they hurried they might miss him. It went against every bone in her body, but she didn't want to come face to face with Ben Matthews this morning and try to be friendly. A simple acknowledgement might be interpreted as unwanted attention.

Her mind was still processing their first meeting last night and she didn't know what to think. All she had wanted was neighbours like the MacKenzies but clearly that wasn't going to happen.

'We're not late, Mum. We're never late,' Jamie huffed, well used to his mother's efficient timekeeping.

'Well we don't want to start today, do we?'

Halfway down the path, her plan to forge ahead was thwarted by Hamish who stopped abruptly and cocked his leg, having found just the right spot for his morning pee, which always took ages. Perfect. Waiting as patiently as she could while Hamish did his business, Eva surreptitiously glanced over at Ben now walking down his garden path. His navy suit looked expensive and showed off his broad chest and long legs but wasn't something she'd expect a university teacher to wear. With Hamish finished they continued down the path where to her surprise, Ben had made a point of waiting for them.

'Morning.'

His tone was formal and his expression uncertain. Part of her hoped he might not be quite as handsome as she remembered last night. But looking at him now she knew there was no chance of that. If anything he was more attractive than she remembered. Unlike the previous evening he was clean-shaven, revealing the shape of a strong jawline, and his dark hair was neatly swept back. Up close Eva noticed he looked tired, but the shadows under his eyes didn't take away from the potency of his gaze.

'Hello,' Eva replied, trying for a nonchalance she wasn't feeling.

'I wanted to thank you for the soup last night – and the heating.' He looked down at the ground and rubbed a hand around the back of his neck, a gesture Eva found annoyingly attractive. Deciding to accept this little interchange as an apology of sorts for his abruptness last night, she returned his smile.

'No problem,' she said, turning to Jamie who was mucking about with Hamish. She looked at him encouragingly. 'Jamie, this is our new neighbour: Ben Matthews. This is my son: Jamie.' She put her hand on his shoulder, unable to keep the pride from her voice.

'Hi, Jamie. Nice to meet you.' He smiled and it was a proper smile that transformed his face – nothing like the scowl he had worn last night Eva noted. She really must have caught him at a bad moment. Ben held out his hand, in a proper man-to-man way, which her son responded to albeit rather self-consciously. Eva watched them. For some inexplicable reason this moment felt significant. She was relieved to see her son act politely but could tell he was eager to be off and meet his friends, his eyes scanning the street. Ben nodded towards the racquet on Jamie's shoulder.

'You play badminton?'

Jamie did a double take now, clearly impressed that their new neighbour, unlike Eva, could recognize a badminton racquet when he saw one.

'Yeah, I go to a club after school,' he explained just before his attention was diverted by a call from one of his friends. 'Fraser's waiting for me, Mum. Remember the trip! I need to know,' he called back as he ran off.

'I will. Be careful! Love you!' The rush of words left her mouth as she watched him go. She turned to Ben and blushed, aware she probably sounded like a madwoman. She cleared her throat. 'So, your first day at the university then?'

He nodded. 'I thought I would use the walk to try and get my bearings.'

'Are you going to the main building or the physics building?'

He shot her a surprised look. 'Um, the physics building.'

'Just walk to the end of this road, turn right onto Doubledykes Road, and take the second left into Kennedy Gardens. From there, you'll start to see university buildings, which are all signposted. You should easily find the physics building.'

'That's helpful, thanks.'

'No problem. Oh, and I returned your house keys this morning through your letterbox. Did you get them?'

'Yes, I did.' He looked down again, his eyes not meeting hers.

On a roll, Eva continued. 'There's also a gap in the fence between our gardens, which I'll come and fix.'

'That's all right, I can get someone in –'

'No, I can do it. I've already got the replacement panels. I just need to measure and cut them to size, then nail them in. Easy.'

He regarded her for a moment before replying. 'Of course. I forgot how practical you are.'

'Good. That's settled then.'

Out of the corner of her eye, Eva saw a familiar car trundling along the road towards them. Eva knew immediately it was Heather who had just dropped Fraser. Grinning like a maniac, she flew by in her people carrier full of assorted children. Not only did she have her own three boys, she was also a childminder and every morning she could be found depositing various children at various locations.

Seeing Eva and Ben, she blasted her car horn, giving a thumbs-up sign. Eva groaned inwardly, hoping Ben didn't see her friend's gesture. 'My friend Heather on the school run,' she explained with a weak laugh just as Hamish, for reasons best known to himself, decided to launch himself at Ben's legs. Thankfully Hamish's front paws only just made contact but enough for two small muddy stains to appear on his trouser leg.

'Oh, I'm so sorry!' Eva looked in horror and without thinking reached to try and brush them off. He held his arm up to stop her, giving her a withering glance.

'It's fine. Please just leave it. I really better get going.' His tone had changed, not that she could blame him. He walked off, leaving Eva to wonder how in such a short space of time she had managed to get off to such a bad start with her new neighbour.

Chapter Three

Eva pulled into the driveway of her mother's house and took a deep breath. She turned to Jamie. 'Here we are then,' she said overbrightly. Jamie pulled off his headphones.

'We're not gonna be long are we, Mum?'

Making the hour-long journey to the leafy Edinburgh suburb to visit her mother wasn't exactly Eva's favourite way to spend a Sunday either but family was family. Her son had already missed out enough losing his father at a young age and Eva was determined he would grow up knowing his grandmother, even if she wasn't exactly fairy-tale material. As for Paul's parents, they grand-parented Jamie the way they had parented their only child. From a great distance and with ridiculous amounts of money being sent at birthdays and Christmas.

'No, we won't be too long. Give Hamish a run around the garden and then bring him back into the car and remember to leave a window open.'

'Why can't he just come in?'

'You know Gran won't have dogs in her house.'

'Come on, Hamish,' Jamie sighed before slouching out of the car door.

Eva pulled a mirror from her bag and quickly checked her reflection. She'd woken early this morning even by her standards, and hadn't been able to get back to sleep, all kinds of strange thoughts whirring through her mind. She went over and over it but couldn't find the thing that seemed to be making her so unsettled. Now her face reflected every minute she had spent pummelling her pillow and tossing and turning. Rummaging in her bag, she found some cream that promised instant radiance, slapped some on her cheeks, and climbed out of the car.

The front door opened and her mother appeared, immaculate as ever. A tailored shift dress with a cashmere cardigan draped over her slim shoulders, Helen Devine was elegant as always. Her blonde hair sat in a neat bob, testament to her weekly visits to the hairdresser's. Eva walked over and leaned in to her mother for a brittle sort of hug, just as Jamie disappeared around the side of the house with Hamish.

'Hello, Mum. How are you?'

'Hello, darling. Come and see my new kitchen!' She clapped her hands together sounding positively giddy as Eva followed her in. As always, the house was neat and orderly. Anything left lying for more than a minute was either dusted or taken away. Dishes, towels, curtains were all coordinated and a crystal cut vase filled with roses always sat on the hall table.

In the kitchen Helen shared the delights of her new Arlington Cream kitchen. Eva trailed after her making appreciative noises as she was shown the joys of the panelled doors, glazed units, and integrated appliances. 'It creates such a beautiful streamline effect, don't you think?' Her mother's eyes sparkled as she looked around at her new kitchen, letting out a contented sigh. She seemed inordinately pleased with herself. In fact, she was looking very well, thought Eva. Narrowing her eyes, she peered closely at her wondering if she had succumbed to a little makeover of her own. There was a definite glow about her.

'It's lovely, Mum,' Eva said, genuinely happy for her. Appearances and status meant everything to Helen. Brian Devine's job as a financial manager had provided his wife with a lifestyle she had taken to very easily and his subsequent life insurance policy had ensured she could keep living it.

Eva walked over to the window and looked out to the garden, thinking how much she still missed her father. A massive heart attack had taken his life and thrown his family's into turmoil. Eva had been working in an insurance office at the time having recently been trusted with the added responsibility of answering the phone as well as doing the filing.

She knew there had to be something more out there, but just hadn't figured out what. As her mother was fond of pointing out, there weren't many opportunities for someone who had left school with not much to show for it. Still, the job gave her enough money to go out with her friends at weekends and buy clothes.

She had met Paul, a ski instructor, the year before on holiday in France. He was handsome, charming, and free-spirited. Eva had a major crush on him, as did most of the girls. She could hardly believe it when he showed interest in her and had been happily swept

40

away by their brief holiday romance. Afterwards, they had kept in touch with the odd phone call or Facebook message.

It had been his idea for Eva to join him in France after her father's death and it hadn't taken much to persuade her. It didn't obviate her pain but it was certainly an effective distraction. Sharing a cramped flat and waitressing long exhausting hours, Eva loved every minute. She relished the freedom and for the first time in her life felt she was having an adventure.

Of course getting pregnant wasn't supposed to be part of the adventure. Suddenly the carefree life she'd been enjoying came crashing down around her – the heady excitement and freedom that had drawn them together becoming something much more real and serious. Paul surprised her by insisting they marry before the baby was born. Marriage was a practical solution to the unplanned turn of events but Eva didn't know if that was enough to base a marriage on. However, she brushed aside her fears knowing it was the right thing to do and it certainly helped to take away some of the terror of being pregnant and having to face her mother.

Her poor mother had barely recovered from Eva going off with Paul in the first place but then had to contend with her youngest daughter returning home three months pregnant to marry in a registry office. Eva nervously clutched her small bouquet of creamy white roses during the short ceremony and afterwards their small party had made their way to a rooftop restaurant where they sat with bowls of steaming mussels overlooking Edinburgh Castle. Eva told herself it was romantic but didn't think her mother would agree judging by her strained expression.

They moved to the Highlands where Paul got a job in the Cairngorms ski resort and lived there until the accident. She hadn't expected things to happen the way they did, but Eva never regretted for a single moment having Jamie in her life.

Staring out of the window Eva could now see him now running around on the neatly clipped lawn with Hamish. The loss of her father and husband had been bad enough but it was Jamie never knowing his grandfather and losing his father that hurt the most. Eva supposed focusing on Jamie had helped her cope with her own grief for Paul and enabled her to move on with her life. Her grief for her father had been harder to deal with – he had been the person she'd looked up to her whole life. He had always been there for her and his absence from her life was still painful. Eva knew if her kind and loving father were still here things would be different somehow and these visits would certainly be easier to deal with.

She closed her eyes and imagined him outside now playing with Jamie. He'd be older obviously, probably retired. His hair would be silver grey but his blue eyes would still be bright and crinkly when he smiled. She could almost hear him laughing as Jamie kicked the ball to him.

Eva inhaled deeply and opened her eyes, surprised to feel tears. She blinked them away just in time to see Hamish happily trampling through a flowerbed and Jamie chasing after him. Eva grimaced, not sure if a crazy dog constituted a suitable male role model for her son. She turned quickly from the window, and pointed to the wall opposite hoping her mother wouldn't notice the damage being inflicted on her garden by Hamish. 'So what are you going to do with this wall?' she asked, moving from the window. Helen looked up from the plate of cocktail-size sausage rolls she was arranging.

'Oh, I need to choose tiles. I'm thinking green or red, something to add a splash of colour.' She smiled, gliding and swooping between her new work surfaces like a graceful ballerina.

'You know, Mum, I could do the tiling for you,' Eva said running her hand over the bare wall.

'Don't be silly, darling. I've got a man coming next week to do it,' Helen replied briskly. Not for the first time Eva wondered if her own determination to master house maintenance skills was a rebound from her mother's inability to change a light bulb without calling in a man. Helen had resumed her preparations for Sunday lunch and turned her attention to making tea.

'What can I do to help?' asked Eva.

'Could you find a plate for these please?' her mother replied nodding towards a tray of freshly baked shortbread fingers sitting on the worktop. Eva started opening the cupboard doors, discovering things had been moved around.

'And how is ... *business*?' she heard Helen ask. Hearing the disdain in her mother's voice never failed to amaze Eva, as if her daughter choosing to run a guest house offended her sensibilities in some way. She had long given up on the hope that her mother might show any real interest or pride in what

Eva had achieved. There was no point in telling her that she had just finished her best season ever, that she already had repeat bookings for next year.

'Business is fine,' she said simply. Finally locating a serving plate Eva arranged the biscuits while Helen spooned tea leaves into a china teapot.

'It's such an odd way to make a living though. Having strangers in your house.'

'Mum, it's St Andrews. They're all respectable paying guests, not exactly strangers.' They'd had this conversation, or one similar to it, several times over the past few years but that didn't make it any less painful.

'But all those people traipsing about your home treating you like some sort of glorified maid,' she continued, giving a little shudder to emphasize her point.

Eva would never deny it was hard work. Guests coming and going, the constant cleaning, laundry and cooking breakfasts. It involved a lot of planning, time, and energy. But living in a big house in a beautiful part of Scotland, running a business that let her be with her son, Eva knew she had much to be thankful for.

Her mother poured milk into a pretty china jug and sighed. 'I just thought you'd have had enough of it by now.' Eva managed to suppress a sigh of her own, thinking nothing had changed since she had moved to St Andrews after Paul had died.

'Will Sarah be coming today?' Eva asked, desperate to change the subject even if it was to Sarah.

'Oh, she'll be here in a minute.' Helen waved her hand vaguely in the air. 'She had to take a call for work.'

'On a Sunday?'

'She's in the middle of an important case. I don't suppose she can switch off just because it's the weekend.'

Sarah was Eva's shiny, perfect older sister. After graduating with a law degree, she had moved to Aberdeen to complete her training in the legal department of an oil company. When their father had died, she moved back to Edinburgh, bought a house practically next door to their mother's, and took a job working for a firm of commercial lawyers. She was always involved in some big case. It wouldn't surprise her if Sarah didn't show up today, just like the last two times Eva and Jamie had visited.

With the tea tray now complete, Helen carried it over to Eva and after a brief inspection of the shortbread biscuits, graced her daughter with a fleeting smile.

'Take this through please, darling,' she said handing over the tray. Eva did as she was told and headed through to the formal dining room where Helen insisted on serving lunch. Heavy cream and gold curtains framed the French doors, which looked out onto the garden, and a rich brocade tablecloth hung over the polished dark wood table where Eva now placed the tray.

'Hello, Eva.'

Eva turned to the sound of her sister's voice. Wearing a crisp white shirt and smart grey trousers and clutching her iPhone, Sarah Devine looked as if she had taken the wrong turning for a business meeting. Beside her, Eva always managed to feel slightly shabby – like the poor relation who had rolled up in skinny jeans and a baggy jumper.

'Hi, Sarah, how are you?' Eva smiled, hesitating for a moment before going over for an awkward embrace.

'Fine. And you?'

'Oh you know, the usual,' she replied overbrightly. 'Jamie should be in any minute. He's out in the garden.'

'I've seen him. He introduced me to your new dog.'

'You met Hamish? He's pretty cute, don't you think?'

Sarah looked at her and raised an eyebrow. 'Do you think getting a dog was a good idea?'

Eva felt a pain start to throb in her head. *No, it probably wasn't a good idea,* she wanted to scream. But she had done it anyway, for Jamie. Eva wondered if her sister ever made an emotional decision or whether everything in her life was calculated on a spreadsheet.

Eva smiled tightly. 'Well, Jamie loves him and it's fun having a dog around the house.' Helen suddenly bustled in, carrying more plates, followed by Jamie.

'Mum! Look what Aunt Sarah got me!' His face a picture of unadulterated joy, he waved an Xbox game in the air: the exact one Eva had planned on giving him as a special Christmas present. Eva swallowed down a burst of anger at her sister. Sarah hadn't seen her nephew in months – she probably didn't even know he had started high school, but in typical style had bought him an expensive present. Couldn't she just spend some time with him, take him to the cinema or something?

46

'That was very generous of her,' Eva said pointedly.

'It was nothing.' Sarah waved her hand casually. Eva took a deep breath and asked Jamie if Hamish was now in the car.

'Yup. And I washed my hands,' he replied.

Now they were all seated at the table, Helen beamed at everyone. 'Isn't this nice? Tuck in, everyone!'

Jamie's eyes hungrily scanned the table and Eva saw his face fall. Plates filled with dainty finger food – quartered sandwiches, scones, and biscuits. Neat tidy food, thought Eva, designed not to leave crumbs. Not like the big spilling-over-the-edge pots of food she made at home. Eva watched her mother's precise delicate movements as she nibbled a sandwich and then glanced over at Sarah who was sipping her tea, barely touching the food.

Eva could swear her mother and sister looked more alike every time she saw them, almost as if they were morphing into the same person, with their neat ice-blonde hair and slender frames. Eva's wavy darker hair and curvier figure only made her feel more of an outsider than she already did. Only the distinctive green eyes they all shared gave any indication the three women were related. Lost in thought, Eva realized her mother was talking to her.

'You remember Gail Worthington from my book club?' Eva didn't but nodded anyway. 'Her daughter Hannah is getting married next year. She's almost forty you know, just goes to show you – it's never too late!'

'That's nice,' Eva replied blandly, presuming the implication being that at thirty-four she still had loads of time to 'find someone'.

'But of course I don't suppose you're likely to meet anyone nice in your line of work are you, darling?' Helen asked doubtfully.

'I meet lots of nice people. I had a professional golfer stay this summer – he took Jamie for a round of golf.'

'A professional golfer?' Helen's face lit up with interest.

'Yes, he was lovely. And so was his wife.' Eva suddenly felt mean, but it always vexed her that her mother seemed intent Eva had to be married off yet somehow it was okay for Sarah to be single, presumably because she had a high-flying career. Of course she felt lonely at times and wished she had someone to share things with. But she also knew if a man ever were to become part of her life again he would have to be so special that he probably didn't exist.

Eva would never admit that to her mother though. No single man in a hundred-mile radius would be safe. Eva almost laughed out loud imagining her mother's reaction if she knew about the handsome physicist now living next door to her.

'And how is the big school, Jamie?'

'S'okay.' He shrugged.

'What's your favourite subject?'

'PE,' Jamie replied brightly.

'Mmmm.' Helen smiled demurely before continuing. 'But you need to work hard at all your subjects, you know. Have you thought yet about what you want to do when you leave school? Things are so competitive these days.' She gave a knowledgeable nod as Jamie looked over to Eva, unsure how to respond.

Eva almost choked on her tea, hardly believing she was hearing the same words that were recited to her over and over when she was in high school.

'I think first year is more about finding his feet and settling in rather than making any career plans,' Eva said through gritted teeth before glancing over at Jamie and giving him a reassuring smile. Of course she wanted him to do well in school but she would never make him feel that was the measure of a successful or happy life.

A silence hung over the table, the only sound Jamie munching his way through most of the food. Eva reached for a scone and spread a thick layer of butter and jam on it before taking a huge bite.

She glanced over at Sarah whose eyes kept flitting to the screen on her precious phone. Eva felt like shouting at her not to be so rude. She wouldn't tolerate Jamie having any electronic gadgets at the table. Eva didn't see why she should be allowed to exclude herself from the conversation and decided it was time she joined in.

'So, Mum says you're working on a big case just now?'

Sarah looked up from her iPhone. 'That's right.'

'So what's it about?'

'It's complicated.' She exhaled. 'Basically a private equity group is suing a law firm for negligence. The case is worth about ten million.'

Eva bristled at her condescending tone. Okay, so her job was important but did she have to act so superior about it?

'Sounds fascinating,' Eva said dryly. Sarah ignored her and smiled at Helen instead.

'Oh, Mum, I changed a few things about in my diary so I'll be able to take you to the chiropodist on Wednesday.'

'This Wednesday?' Eva jumped in. 'I could take you, Mum. What time is it at?'

Helen shook her head. 'No it's fine. Sarah's taken me before so she knows where to go.'

Eva bit her lip thinking nothing had changed. Ever since they were little girls Sarah had always sought their mother's approval. Eva had always been closer to her father, preferring to stay with him pottering in the garden or helping him do little jobs while Helen and Sarah favoured shopping.

With most of the food finished thanks to Jamie and Eva, Helen turned her attention to Jamie again.

'Now, Jamie, come and spend some time with me before your mum whisks you away again.' The remark wasn't lost on Eva, managing to make it sound as if she never saw him even though she visited as often as possible and was constantly inviting her to visit.

Jamie dutifully followed Helen out of the room, throwing Eva an accusing look as he went. She ruffled his hair as he passed and started to collect plates from the table, glancing over to see Sarah's manicured fingers tapping furiously away. Eva assumed it was business but then what did she know? Maybe she was arranging a romantic rendezvous with a secret lover. She knew so little about her sister's life these days.

How and when it had got to this stage she didn't know. Their personalities had always been different but once they had been close. Eva remembered the two giggling girls hiding behind the curtains waiting for their dad to come home. Or the teenagers sitting up late into the night discussing what boys they fancied at school. Everything changed after their dad's heart attack. Instead of bringing them closer, it had seemed to tear them apart.

Sarah showed no signs of helping to clear the table and Eva felt a rush of anger.

'Surely it can wait, whatever it is?' she snapped. Sarah jumped slightly and looked up. Eva could see slight shadows beneath her sister's expensive make-up and immediately felt guilty.

'Is everything all right?' she asked her.

'Yes, why shouldn't it be?'

'No reason. I just thought you looked tired.'

'Well that's what happens when you work a fifty-hour week,' Sarah replied sarcastically. Eva took a deep breath, willing herself to stay calm. Eva knew very well what it was like, but of course Sarah would never acknowledge that.

'Maybe you could take a break after this case,' Eva suggested.

'Maybe.' She sniffed. 'It will depend on my work schedule and I can't just leave Mum.'

'Why not?' Eva asked surprised.

'She's not getting any younger you know.'

'She looks fine to me. More than fine, in fact. Is there a problem I don't know about?'

'No,' Sarah replied defensively. 'She just needs to know I'm here, that's all. I can't just take off.'

'But I'm here for her too! I'm only an hour away and she could come and stay with me if she wanted.' Eva had lost count of the times she had invited her mother to come to St Andrews. She glared at Sarah and then shook her head in despair. Balancing a pile of plates in her arms she carried them through to the kitchen, not trusting herself to speak.

She plonked the dishes down and began to stack the dishwasher. She took a few calming breaths, suddenly overwhelmed with sadness. She couldn't bear the thought of her and Sarah spending the next few years fighting like this every time they met until eventually they wouldn't bother to see each other at all. Maybe if they could see each other in different circumstances and relax, they would have a chance to fix whatever it was that was broken between them.

She thought of Jamie's trip in a couple of weeks. Deep down she knew she'd have to agree to let him go. Until she actually told him though, she felt she still had some control. Once he knew he was going there would be no turning back. She couldn't even imagine what she would do with herself that weekend. Before she could change her mind, she went back to the dining room.

'I was thinking, Sarah – Jamie's got a trip coming up at the end of November – one of those activity weekends for kids. There's rock climbing, abseiling … that type of thing. I'm a bit nervous about it to be honest, the thought of him doing all those things.' Eva forced a little laugh, not feeling natural to be confiding in her sister.

'Anyway, why don't you come up to St Andrews that weekend? There are some great restaurants. We could go for a few walks, maybe open a few bottles of wine. I think there's even a winter market on that weekend.'

Sarah looked at her blankly. 'Sorry, what? Oh no, I'll be busy that weekend.'

'But I didn't even say which – you know, it doesn't matter.' Eva felt her shoulders slump, suddenly deflated. She gathered the linen napkins from the table, absently admiring the orchid design on them.

'I'd better go and find Jamie and Mum,' she muttered, not waiting to hear if Sarah replied. In the gleaming new kitchen Eva stood helplessly for a moment. She wished she didn't have to leave feeling this way. She told herself she'd be home soon, home to her sanctuary. But even that didn't feel the same any more without the MacKenzies being there. A sudden image of Ben Matthews came into her head and she found herself wondering how he was spending his Sunday.

***

Ben had woken late on Sunday, surprised he had slept for so long. In the kitchen he looked out of the window at the inky grey sky and wondered if it rained here every day. Realizing he was hungry he took eggs from the fridge, deciding to make an omelette. After he had eaten maybe he would go for a walk, explore the town some more. He could buy a paper and come back and read it at leisure.

It still felt odd having Sundays free. Every Sunday for the past five years he had visited his mother at Cartvale care home. He tried but usually failed to fit in a midweek visit too if work allowed. But he would always spend the whole Sunday with her no matter what. If she was having a good day, they'd walk in the local park or perhaps even have lunch somewhere.

In some ways, Ben had started to grieve for his mother years before she actually died. The strong woman who had brought him up alone after his father had died started to disappear long before her diagnosis of early onset Alzheimer's. Yet even now at odd moments like this, the grief and guilt could creep up on him, its severity taking him by surprise. He took a deep breath, sloshing hot water over the coffee granules in a mug, determined not to go there.

In the dining room – now Ben's makeshift office – he cleared a space on the table for his plate and ate hungrily. He flicked through a few of the papers and books in front of him, his mound of reading to catch up on. His meeting at the university had gone well on Friday. Meeting up with Professor Drummond had felt like reclaiming something valuable from his old life.

A slightly eccentric Scot, he had guided Ben through his PhD at Oxford University with patience, wisdom, and more than the odd dram of whisky. Ben had respected him so much and always felt he had let him down in some way, turning his back on research and going to work as an analyst in the city.

But the Professor had never passed judgement and had understood Ben's need to earn the type of money you couldn't earn in academia. Ben hadn't been surprised when he discovered his old Professor was now at St Andrews, the oldest university in Scotland. An image of him came to Ben's mind, sitting by a roaring fire with a tumbler in hand. But Ben knew his Professor's easy charm was matched by his ferocious intelligence. He was still at the forefront of research into gravitational waves. Ben had read his recently published paper, and knew he wanted to be part of it again.

He had responded to Ben's email with all the enthusiasm Ben remembered. They both knew it wasn't an obvious or easy option to return to academia from the world of finance but in typical style Professor Drummond had seen it as a positive, not a negative. 'Be good to get some fresh blood into the place, a new perspective. Things can get a bit stuffy in academia.'

After several exchanged emails, Ben had a formal interview via Skype with the Professor and two of his colleagues in the department. He had been questioned in detail about his plans for research – and more importantly, what funding he would obtain. He had listed the grants he could apply for, what journals he would publish in. Ben had studied the curriculum and courses on offer for students and expressed his willingness to be flexible, happy to fit in with the department's teaching requirements but also had some ideas of his own about teaching.

When the Professor had phoned offering him a position, Ben felt exhilarated. The realization that he wasn't going back to working in the City came as a relief but he didn't underestimate what lay ahead of him. Ben and Professor Drummond had chatted as they walked around the university grounds, Ben admiring the ivy-clad buildings and absorbing the buzz of students milling around. He had been shown around the department and introduced to a few people.

They'd agreed Ben would start with a few hours' teaching next week before going full-time the following week. Until then Ben would take some time to acclimatize to his new surroundings. Finishing his breakfast Ben stood up, leaving the dishes on the table. He'd start with a walk on the beach.

Chapter Four

Eva was nursing a cup of tea. She stared at her phone, an air of gloom still hanging over her after seeing her mum and sister yesterday. The day was chilly and damp and she pulled her cardigan tightly around her. Thinking back to the strained atmosphere between her and Sarah, she debated with herself whether to text her or not.

She let out a deep sigh. It was ridiculous to feel so unsure about contacting her own sister. Maybe she should just forget the whole thing, pretend everything was fine until the next time. But deep down it pained her. She wanted at least to be on civil terms with Sarah.

Memories of her father had also been haunting her, as was often the case after being in her old home – almost as if her grief had been renewed in some way. It wasn't just the physical pain of missing him, the horrible gaping hole he'd left in her life. It was her disappointment and frustration that he'd never see what she had achieved.

Eva gave herself a little shake. All this indecisiveness was no good. Before she could regret it, she tapped out a message to Sarah repeating her offer to stay for a weekend and pressed send. Eva startled as Hamish suddenly let out a bark at the sound of the doorbell ringing.

Seeing Greg Ritchie standing on her doorstep wasn't the most welcome sight but Eva summoned a smile. 'Hello, Greg.'

'Eva, hi. How are you?' He flashed a dazzling smile.

'I'm very well, thanks. And you?'

'Good, good. Could I have a minute of your time?'

Eva widened the door holding on to Hamish's collar and allowing Greg to pass. She suppressed a little shudder as he stepped in. Something about Greg Ritchie's practised smooth manner always made her feel uneasy. He had certainly found a look and stuck with it, she thought, acknowledging his customary well-cut suit, polished shoes, and slicked-back hair.

The owner of one of the largest hotels in St Andrews, he had been one of the first people to introduce himself to Eva, offering to 'show her the ropes'. He had insisted she accompany him to a networking event. 'It's important to keep in touch with other businesspeople – share ideas and give support,' he'd told her.

Leaving Jamie with Moira next door, Eva had dressed in the plain black dress she had worn for Paul's funeral, the only thing she had remotely suitable for such an event. Waiting for Greg to collect her, she had felt nervous and like a fraud. She wasn't a proper businesswoman; at least she didn't feel like one then. She was a widow who had bought a huge house and was feeling totally out of her depth. She'd spent most of the evening standing nervously in the corner and couldn't help admire the way Greg worked the room, shaking hands and chatting easily to people.

He seemed to know all the jargon and buzzwords, which sounded like a foreign language to Eva. It had been terrifying making conversation with strangers but somehow she'd got through it, leaving with a handful of business cards and knowing a few new faces.

Since then, there'd been a host of things for Eva to get to grips with. Finding the right suppliers, registering with the tourist board, getting to grips with marketing and running a website. Every now and again, Greg descended upon her with these little visits for no particular reason Eva could fathom. She was pretty sure – at least she hoped – Greg's motives were well intentioned but she had instinctively kept her distance from him.

Clearly he was an astute businessman and a serious networker but his reputation with women wasn't something Eva wanted to experience first-hand. He was certainly handsome in an obvious way and from what she'd heard there was no shortage of women who appreciated his particular brand of charm.

But he was way too smooth for Eva – there was a fine line between charm and smarm. Like his five-star hotel, everything about him was a little too polished and posed for Eva's taste – his silky smile always at the ready. A snapshot of the one and only smile she'd seen from Ben Matthews popped into her head – where on earth had that come from?

Giving herself a little shake Eva followed Greg into the hall where he was looking around with an appraising air. Eva had the sudden image of a big over-friendly dog coming to mark his territory in some way.

'Can I get you something, Greg? A drink?' she asked.

'No time thanks,' he replied. His eyes flicked to his smartphone as though something vitally important could come through any second and Eva thought he might get on well with Sarah.

'You know there's a big conference at the university in a couple of weeks?'

'Sure,' Eva lied. One of the benefits of not opening in winter was not having to be up to speed with every event in the town.

'Six hundred delegates arriving for two nights – obviously we're fully booked. But I've experienced a few er, technical issues with our new booking system leaving me with two guests and no rooms to offer them. I'd like to be able to tell them I've made arrangements for alternative accommodation.' He gave her a silky smile. 'And of course, I thought of you. I know you close in winter but I was hoping I could rely on you to take two guests for a couple of nights?'

For some reason the thought of his slick operation not running smoothly made Eva want to giggle but she knew she would agree. It wasn't just that she wanted to help – of course she did. Nor was it for the extra income even though it would be welcome. If she was honest, she jumped at the chance of having something to do. Jamie's longer days at school left her with more time on her hands and, alarmingly, she was discovering the joys of daytime television. The theme music to *Bargain Hunt* was beginning to sound oddly comforting and Eva didn't think that was a good thing.

'Of course, that won't be a problem. Would you like me to contact them directly?'

He nodded in confirmation. 'I'll let them know we've got accommodation and I'll email you with their details. That all right with you?'

'Sure, that's fine with me.'

With that sorted Greg looked about with an approving air.

'So, your place is looking good, Eva,' he commented.

'Er, thanks.'

'You have a good summer season?'

'Really good, yes.'

'Still suits you to close in winter?' He raised a quizzical eyebrow.

'Um, yes –'

Greg pounced on her split-second hesitation.

'So you would consider opening all year?'

'That's not what I –'

'There's plenty of business out there you know,' he interrupted. 'Lots of people choosing staycations. Scotland is a top destination – St Andrews is thriving. In the next couple of months alone there's jazz, poetry, and film festivals ... hundreds of visitors all looking for a nice place to stay.' He was pacing up and down now, getting into his stride, his pungent aftershave wafting about after him.

'Well, it's not really –' Eva began.

'Have you ever thought about expanding?'

'Expanding?' Eva blinked.

'You could get a drinks licence, serve food, open all year round ... There's a lot of potential here. For example, what special offers do you run?'

'Depending on how busy it is, I sometimes offer three for two nights.' He seemed to dismiss that with a wave of his hand.

'You could do much more. St Andrew's Day is coming up, Burns Night – all good for winter trade. Some guest houses tie in with the golf courses – offer three nights with three rounds of golf, that type of thing.'

Eva nodded her head, making interested but non-committal noises.

'If it's the financial side of things you're concerned about, I'd be more than happy to discuss investment opportunities. Perhaps we could discuss it over dinner one night?'

Eva rubbed her temple feeling like she'd stepped on a runaway train and needed to figure out how to stop it. She straightened her shoulders and mustered her firmest voice. 'It's really not something I'm thinking about at the moment, Greg. But thanks anyway.' She took a step towards the front door indicating for him to follow.

'No need to make any decisions just now. Have a think about it.' He patted her arm, gracing her with a final smile as he left.

Eva felt odd after she'd shown Greg out. He hadn't told her anything she didn't already know but his words rattled about uncomfortably in her head. Recently, some part of her brain – the part that knew it would make financial sense as well as fill her days – had been mulling over the possibility of opening in winter. But another part of her brain simply refused to contemplate the change. Did she really want guests in her house the whole year round? But one thing she was sure of, whatever happened she certainly wouldn't be discussing anything with Greg Ritchie and becoming one of his pet projects or anything else for that matter.

Returning to the kitchen she reached for her laptop, wincing as she took a mouthful of now cold tea. Once she received the guests' details from Greg she'd send emails confirming their reservations. She clicked on the university website and found the conference Greg had mentioned: a major event with delegates arriving from all over the world. She scanned through the information, reading out loud as she scrolled down. 'International Science Conference ... bringing together leading scientists ... guest speakers ... workshops, coffee breaks, evening receptions ...'

The itinerary looked full so it was unlikely her guests would be lingering at the guest house. Even so, she would make them feel as comfortable as possible. It wasn't for another couple of weeks but Eva was happy to have something to focus on and decided to give the bedrooms a quick tour of inspection.

Opening the door to the newly decorated coastal-theme bedroom, Eva was pleased with the final result. She just had the bedding to choose and she took a mental note to add some fresh flowers before the guests arrived. She moved across the hallway to the bedroom at the back of the house, which overlooked the garden. Here, Eva had taken her inspiration from the time she'd lived in the Highlands. The walls were painted pale green and a reupholstered tartan armchair – one of her finds in a second-hand shop –

sat by the fireplace. A few pots with sprigs of purple heather and a painting of the Cairngorm mountains completed the room that American tourists loved.

Eva headed back downstairs noticing the post had been delivered. She smiled when she saw the postcard on the doormat, already knowing it was from Moira and Donald. Eva wondered where they were now as she bent down to pick it up. She found something charming and old-fashioned about Moira going to the effort of writing and sending postcards. She liked to imagine her with her usual gin and tonic, sitting down to write while looking out on some glorious ocean view.

They were having the time of their lives by the sound of it. Moira wrote about the places they'd visited, describing the rugged beauty of New Zealand's mountains and seeing the bubbling hot springs in Japan. Now they were sailing to Hong Kong.

Seeing the familiar handwriting Eva felt a pang of regret that she wasn't able to pop next door and have a chat. She sighed, wondering if she would ever travel like that. She and Jamie had never had a proper holiday. During summer Eva couldn't leave the business and at other times Jamie was at school. It wasn't just the lack of time; it was also the money. After day-to-day living, most of the profit Eva made went back into the guest house to keep it in tip-top shape. Customers' ability to browse, choose, and review online meant Eva had to compete with the best to keep securing business.

After reading the postcard, she pinned it to the fridge in the kitchen along with the others. Deciding to make fresh tea, she filled the kettle and leaned against the worktop for a moment. The kitchen, a large bright space, was the hub of her home and Eva's favourite place in the house. One end of the kitchen was taken up by stainless steel appliances and was organized in accordance with various health and safety regulations for food preparation.

At the other end Eva had created a homely, cosy space for her and Jamie, which was dominated by a wooden table. A small French dresser stood in one corner crammed with recipe books, ceramic pots, and dried flowers in bright vases. Drawings from Jamie's nursery days were pinned to the wall alongside various photographs.

Waiting for the kettle to boil, Eva checked the large cupboard outside the kitchen where she kept all her supplies. The top shelf was packed with toiletries for the guest rooms and the bottom shelves were stacked with clean linen and towels. Feeling suddenly restless, Eva wanted to get on with something. Tea forgotten, she decided to make a start on the en suites and reached for a pile of white fluffy towels.

As she passed Hamish sleeping off their earlier walk, he opened one eye and looked up at her. Mrs Duffy was lovely but Eva wished there was some way of speeding up the training process. She chuckled to herself, thinking there should be some kind of doggy boot camp for disobedient dogs. 'What am I going to do with you when the guests are here?' she asked Hamish. But his only response was to thump his tail lazily on the floor before closing his eyes again. Clearly he wasn't too concerned with such matters.

***

Ben walked home pleased his first few days at the university had gone well and in particular the first lecture he'd given this morning. Standing in the lecture theatre in front of a hundred students had been both terrifying and exhilarating. After introducing himself, his nerves had settled and he'd got into his stride, hopefully giving his students a better understanding of Newton's Laws of Motion. He took it as a good sign when students' hands shot up at the end to ask questions. He'd then spent an hour with two first-year students going over an advanced mathematics topic and was rewarded by seeing realization dawn on their faces as they started to understand three-dimensional integrals.

His work at the university might be going well but he couldn't say the same for his new house. With each day that passed, the sense that he was neglecting it grew. So much about the house was perfect but in the cold light of day he could see the cracks showing, quite literally. Only this morning he'd noticed where rainwater had seeped in through his bedroom window.

As he unlocked the front door he tried to shake the feeling he was an imposter letting himself into someone else's house. Ben stood still for a moment in the hall, sensing something wasn't right. Following a faint sound through to the front living room, he looked up to see a small ominous bulge surrounded by an ugly brown stain protruding from a corner of the ceiling. A slow steady drip of water fell onto the carpet.

He swore under his breath. Just what he needed. A leak – but what the hell should he do? He knew enough to find the stopcock under the kitchen sink and turn off the water. He looked around helplessly for something to catch the water. In his London flat he'd make one phone call to his landlord and it would all be sorted. But things were different here.

He managed to find a pan and grabbed it to place it under the drip, wondering what to do next. The thought of starting to phone around random engineers wasn't appealing. His mind turned to Eva, remembering she had the name of someone – what choice did he have?

Moments later he knocked on Eva's shiny blue front door and as he waited for her to answer he looked properly at her house for the first time. In comparison to his more formal front garden, hers was rambling and full of colour. Fragrant purple lavender and flowering shrubs lined the path and pots filled with small creamy flowers stood either side of the front door.

Eva opened the door holding a pile of white towels, with her hair piled high and a few loose tendrils framing her face. Ben swallowed hard. Did this woman ever look anything less than adorable? And what the hell was happening to him? Standing there, he'd almost forgotten why he was here.

'Hi.'

Her smile was tentative and her voice held a cautious note. Hamish appeared at Eva's legs, took one look at

Ben, and let out a low growl before shooting out to the front garden. Clearly Ben hadn't made a very good first impression on him either. Ben saw Eva's startled expression before she thrust the towels into his chest.

'Hold these,' she ordered and ran off in pursuit of her wayward dog. Hamish circled the front garden several times, enjoying the impromptu game of chase before finally sensing perhaps his mistress wasn't pleased with him. Ben watched helplessly from the doorway wondering if he should be helping in some way. Thankfully Hamish appeared to calm down and was now being led back to the house by his collar.

'Sorry about that,' Eva said with a weak smile, looking slightly harassed.

'No, no – I'm sorry. I didn't mean to cause any difficulties ...'

'It's not your fault,' she sighed, casting a disappointed look at Hamish. 'And I'm sorry about him jumping up on you the other day. We've only had him a few weeks and we're still training him.' She reached to take the towels back from Ben.

'It's fine; please don't worry.' He bent down patting Hamish on his head, hoping the gesture would reassure him – and Eva – that he wasn't really such a terrible person.

'Anyway, is there anything I can do for you?'

He straightened up to find Eva's direct gaze on him. 'Well, I was wondering if you had the name of a plumber? There seems to be a problem –'

'Is your heating not working again?'

'I'm not sure what the problem is to be honest. I think there must to be a leak somewhere. Water's coming from the ceiling in the front room.'

'Let me settle Hamish and get my tools. I'll be round in a minute.' She appeared immediately more relaxed now she was able to help. Ben hadn't expected her to actually come round but now realized he wasn't that surprised. Within a few minutes she was taking control of the situation and issuing instructions.

'I'll need to turn on all your cold taps just to let the water run to reduce the pressure. The water's fresh-looking so it's likely to be a pipe from the upstairs en suite.' Ben could only look on in silent admiration as Eva went to work, seeming to know exactly what to do.

A while later when Eva had finished and with disaster averted, Ben made tea and brought it through to the front room where Eva stood surveying the room.

'Thanks,' she murmured as he handed her a mug. He wondered what she was thinking. His only contribution to the room was the marble-topped sideboard, coffee table, and two leather sofas he'd brought from London. He'd told the removal men to dump them anywhere and that's exactly what they had done. He remembered the day Samantha had dragged him to an Italian designer shop to buy them. They had been hideously expensive. In his London apartment he imagined them to look smart and sophisticated. Here, set against the floral wallpaper and patterned blue carpet, they looked so ridiculous he had a sudden urge to laugh.

'It's such a lovely room,' Eva said wistfully as if she was imagining how it could look. Her eyes swept the room and Ben followed her gaze up to the newly damaged ceiling.

'The brown stain really lends a certain something, don't you think?' he said.

Eva's head spun round, looking at him with a quizzical frown. Their eyes met and held before they both laughed, the atmosphere between them suddenly relaxing.

'Well, obviously it needs some attention.' Eva smiled.

'I won't argue with you there,' Ben replied ruefully.

'They are big houses. It's going to take you a while to get it the way you want it.'

Ben muttered vaguely in agreement.

'Have you thought about what you'd like to do with this room?' Eva asked. Ben lifted his mug to his mouth, thinking how he didn't even know if he'd be staying in the house, let alone decorating it.

'Not really. Decorating, interiors … they're not really my thing,' he replied feeling slightly awkward.

'What about your last house where you lived – London you said?'

'I think the term functional would cover it,' Ben said dryly. 'It was rented and I didn't really spend that much time in it.' His London flat had been a place to eat and sleep but he'd wanted so much more for this house. He saw Eva shoot him a curious look. He could see the questions in her eyes that she was too polite to ask. What was he doing in this big house on his own?

For one mad moment he almost blurted it out. He could tell her that at the grand age of thirty-four he was on his own. No family, no partner, no special person. And it suddenly hit him just how alone he was. He might have a bank account with more money than he knew how to spend and an impressive list of qualifications but he was still on his own. He'd envisaged him and Samantha turning this into a proper family home but that was before he realized it was a one-sided dream.

The way Eva was looking at him made him feel it would be so easy to speak to her, to confide in her. But he stopped in time, reminding himself that he didn't want to get involved. Polite but distant, that was his strategy. Why he needed a strategy he didn't know but something about this woman was getting under his skin and one thing he did know was that he didn't need the distraction. It would be crazy for him to get close to his new neighbour, he told himself. Yet here he was finding himself drawn towards her, noticing her in a way that probably wasn't wise.

Eva had moved over to the wall. 'Our houses have the same basic layout but next door's had a few adjustments made for the business. I love these front rooms overlooking the beach. There's so much light and space and it's east-facing so it's lovely in the morning,' she said, patting the wall in a knowledgeable manner. 'It's structurally sound, but Donald's – Mr MacKenzie's – arthritis meant they hadn't done much to the house in the last few years. But it could look amazing.'

Ben, leaning against the doorframe, gave himself a mental shake realizing he'd become slightly transfixed watching Eva Harris who was looking at him expecting some sort of response. He straightened up and cleared his throat.

'Had they lived here long?'

'Oh yes, for years,' she told him, her face brightening as she talked about her old neighbours. 'Their children were born and brought up in this house and they still lived here after they retired but it just got too much for them. They're moving into a bungalow near their son once they come back from their cruise.'

'Sounds as if they were happy here.'

'They were. It's a house full of lovely memories.' She smiled. 'Every year they had a big Christmas party, invited practically the whole street.' Seeing her expression Ben thought she might well be wishing they hadn't left.

'And you? Have you lived here long?' he asked her.

'Seven years. I moved here after my husband died. Jamie was four at the time.' She spoke matter-of-factly, clearly not looking for sympathy yet Ben felt a surge of something. He wasn't sure what the feeling was. There was no doubt she was a strong, independent woman but knowing she had lost her husband and obviously at a young age gave her a vulnerability.

'I'm sorry. That must have been tough.'

She nodded thoughtfully. 'It was – especially at the beginning. But then Jamie started school, I got the business up and running, and the MacKenzies ... well, they helped me so much. Very soon it felt like home. I came to realize home isn't necessarily where you were born or grew up. It's about knowing you simply don't want to be anywhere else.'

Ben listened to her words, and knew he had never felt that way about a place. Eva drained the last of her tea and Ben watched as she started to gather up her tools, once again finding himself slightly in awe of her practical abilities.

'Anyway, it's the start of winter so there are probably a few checks you should be doing. I've tightened the valve in the pipework so that'll do for now but you should really get a plumber in to have a look at it.' She checked her watch. 'I'd better get going. Jamie will be home from school soon.'

'Of course.'

Eva headed out to the hall and remembering something, turned to Ben.

'I told you I don't normally open the guest house in winter but I have two guests arriving at the beginning of December – only for a couple of nights though.'

Ben smiled in response. 'Thanks for letting me know.'

'One of the hotels messed up their bookings and asked me to help out – they're here for a conference at the university,' she told him as she zipped up her toolbag.

'That'll probably be the International Science Conference?' Ben raised a questioning eyebrow.

'Yeah, I think that's the one; at least it's the only one I could see when I checked the university website. Is that something you'll be involved in?'

Ben nodded. 'There's a few talks and workshops I want to attend plus the Professor in my department is a keynote speaker so I'll definitely go to that.'

At the front door Ben ran a hand through his hair, thanking her again. 'I seem to be making a habit of this.'

'Sorry?'

'Relying on you for help.'

She shrugged. 'I'm happy to help. That's what neighbours are for.'

Ben closed the front door and shook his head, wondering why the house suddenly felt so empty again.

Chapter Five

There might be better ways to spend a Monday morning, but right now Ben couldn't think of any. Finding himself with a free morning he'd decided to take a walk and after leaving his house it had only taken him a few minutes to reach West Sands beach. He inhaled deeply, savouring the sharp salty sea air and enjoying the touch of winter sun on his face. He strolled along with the expanse of sparkling water beside him and only the squabbling seagulls overhead for company.

In London, he would have been at his desk for hours by now, checking the *FT* and *Bloomberg* to see if anything had moved in the market overnight followed by meetings to discuss major trades and which clients to involve. If he was lucky he'd manage to grab a sandwich at his desk while keeping an eye on six screens.

Life was going to be different from now on and he was filled with a sense of wellbeing, an unexpected surge of joy for life. He was discovering it wasn't actually the worst thing in the world to get to know your neighbour, not when she came in the shape and form of Eva Harris anyway. To smile at each other, exchange a few words, maybe even give a wave in passing.

Ben had formed the impression that Eva Harris liked to keep busy. Yesterday he'd noticed the fence between their back gardens had been mended. He imagined her hammering away with her tools and the thought made him smile.

When he came home from work, he'd see lights on in her house making it look warm and inviting. More than could be said about his own house. He seemed incapable of summoning the energy to do anything and most of the boxes remained unopened, a miserable reminder of his inability to make a decision about what to do. The house was beginning to feel like a burden, a symbol of everything he had got so wrong with Samantha. He might be able to calculate complicated mathematical equations but he wasn't so sure about his ability to judge relationships.

The dreams that had brought him to St Andrews, of settling with a loving family, still lingered but he now knew and accepted it wasn't going to happen with Samantha – in fact, he had trouble even imagining her here now. The house was a huge project and just the thought of it overwhelmed him and zapped his energy. Maybe he should buy somewhere smaller and simply concentrate on his job. But turning his back on the house would be tantamount to giving up on those same dreams and he wasn't sure if he was ready to do that.

An unbidden thought at the very back of his mind acknowledged Eva's presence in his life. He couldn't figure out why but every time he contemplated the house or what he should do next, she crept into his thoughts. Somehow he knew she could make this house a home so easily but why he was even thinking like that left him baffled. He shook his head, reminding himself she was a widow, a single mum with a business to run – all baggage he didn't want to handle. Focus on work and nothing else, he told himself taking another deep breath.

A dog's yapping pulled his thoughts to the present. Just ahead of him a small dog played at the water's edge, barking excitedly as it chased the ripples. Ben blinked, realizing he recognized the dog. He scanned the horizon until he saw Eva's figure coming towards them, calling Hamish's name and squeaking a toy. The dog was totally ignoring her. What was it with that woman and animals?

As she drew nearer, his eyes ran appreciatively over her body. She was wearing a pink anorak, a colourful scarf around her neck, and black leggings that revealed a pair of shapely legs. So much for focusing on work and nothing else.

'Hamish, here, now!' she called in a stern voice. Finally reaching Hamish, she leaned down, snapped the lead onto his collar, and looked up at Ben.

'Oh, hi! I didn't realize it was you.' She spoke slightly breathlessly, her cheeks flushed and eyes sparkling. She looked so free and natural Ben could hardly tear his eyes away from her. He looked down at Hamish to distract himself from the thoughts suddenly racing through his mind.

'Training going well?' He grinned.

'A work in progress I think you'd call it.' She laughed. 'Jamie and I have been working on his recall but as you can see, it's a bit hit and miss. But we'll get there, won't we, Hamish?' She patted the dog affectionately.

'You have your hands full with this one.' Ben crouched down to Hamish who took the opportunity to roll over and have his belly rubbed.

'He's enjoying that.' Eva grinned.

Ben straightened up, gesturing to their surroundings. 'Well, he's certainly a lucky dog living here.'

'So you're enjoying the beach?'

'Very much,' he replied truthfully. 'It's beautiful.'

As they continued to walk companionably along the sand, he glanced sideways at her. 'Is this usually how you start your day?'

'In winter, yes. I think there's something special about it at this time of year.'

He saw her take a deep breath and look around, her love for her surroundings plain to see. 'But summer is a different story. Round about this time in the morning you'll find me knee-deep in teas, coffees, and making breakfasts for guests.'

Ben smiled, vague memories infiltrating his mind of holidays at the seaside with his parents. One day he'd got lost among the crowds on the beach. It had probably been only for a few minutes but it had felt like a lifetime and he'd never forgotten the look on his mother's face when she found him, eyes shiny with tears of relief.

'My parents took me to Morecambe a few times,' he told Eva. 'You know the kind of holiday – playing crazy golf, eating ice-cream on a freezing beach.' He narrowed his eyes as he recollected. 'We stayed in this small bed and breakfast on the seafront. We were all crammed into a tiny bedroom and for some reason I can remember the creaky staircase. In the morning we'd have to be in the dining room at some outrageously early time or else the landlady refused to serve breakfast.'

Eva chuckled. 'Well, guest houses have changed a lot since then. Customers are very discerning these days and us landladies have to be a bit more accommodating.'

'But I bet people still want a traditional fry-up for breakfast?'

'Not so much these days. Guests want everything from soya yogurt to vegetarian sausages.' She rolled her eyes in mock exasperation. 'Then after breakfast I do laundry, clean, maybe help guests plan their day.'

'Sounds busy.'

She nodded in agreement. 'In fact, I recently calculated this summer I made breakfast for 420 guests, cleaned 219 bathrooms, and did 370 laundry loads.'

He laughed. 'Really? That's impressive. You do all that by yourself?'

'The MacKenzies' granddaughter used to help me out. She often stayed with them during summer and was happy to earn some pocket money.'

'And the guests – what are they like?'

'Usually great. About seventy per cent is repeat business. Golfers and holidaymakers mostly and of course graduation time is busy. There's the occasional difficult customer but mostly I enjoy it, and it means I can be here for Jamie.'

Ben could see her face soften when she mentioned her son, her devotion to him obvious. He admired her for the way she just seemed to get on with it. Running a business on her own couldn't be easy. As they headed towards the grassy dunes Ben could see the Royal and Ancient Golf Club, a grand-looking building overlooking the first tee of the famous golf course.

They fell into step behind Hamish who was forging ahead, straining on the lead despite Eva's attempts to bring him to heel beside her. They were now on the main street, which Ben noted had a pleasing absence of big-name high street shops. Instead there was an eclectic mix of gift shops, galleries, and food sellers, their windows displaying ceramics, antiques, and hand-made chocolate.

'I can see why so many people come to St Andrews; it certainly seems to have plenty to offer.'

Eva seemed pleased that he liked it, her smile widening.

'And there's so much more to it. The aquarium is nearby and there's the castle, the cathedral, and the botanic gardens are really lovely ...' Her voice trailed off. 'Sorry, I've just realized I'm giving you my tourist spiel – force of habit.'

'Not at all. Once I'm settled, I hope to have time to visit all those places,' Ben replied. 'I assume it's much busier in summer though?'

Eva nodded in agreement. 'It can get really busy especially when the golf is on.'

A cool breeze had picked up and the sky had turned grey, holding the threat of rain. They walked on in silence for a few moments, each with their own thoughts until Eva spoke.

'Now the best part of my morning walk.' She pointed to a pretty coffee shop with a striped blue and white awning hanging over the window and a sign above the door bearing the name *The Coffee Hut*.

'The coffee's pretty good if you'd like to join me.' She looked at him, her voice tentative.

'I think I could manage a coffee.' Ben smiled.

Warmth, chatter, and the scent of fresh coffee surrounded them as they entered the shop. Large squashy sofas and low wooden tables created a relaxed feel to the place. While the back wall consisted of exposed brickwork, the other walls were each painted a different colour and held various pieces of artwork. Tempting cakes and pastries were displayed on the counter and the coffee machine hissed and steamed comfortingly in the background. Small lamps and vases of flowers were dotted about and Ben immediately understood why Eva would like coming here after her walk.

A few people were hunched over their laptops and a couple of mothers with toddlers sat chatting, while a group of students gathered round a table talked animatedly. Ben joined Hamish who seemed to know the routine and had settled under a table while Eva went to organize the coffee. Ben sat back taking in his surroundings but his eyes kept skipping over to Eva where she stood at the counter talking and laughing with the woman making the coffees.

'Looks like a nice place,' he commented as she returned with a tray to their table.

'The owners – Jack and Freya – started their business around the same time as me. I suppose we've helped and encouraged each other along the way.' Eva placed mugs of hot frothy coffee on their table along with a delicious-looking pastry.

'That was Freya I was talking to although it's usually Jack you'll see running this place. Freya is an artist – these are all her paintings on the walls.'

Ben turned his head to regard the paintings. His knowledge of art was non-existent but it was easy to see the appeal of the vibrant, colourful seascapes.

'I display a few of Freya's paintings in my rooms and likewise Freya and Jack are happy to recommend my guest house,' Eva explained biting into her pastry with obvious relish. 'Sorry, I haven't eaten breakfast this morning.'

Ben looked away, the sight of her wiping crumbs from her mouth stirring something deep within him.

'So no more leaks I hope?' she asked brightly.

Ben lifted his cup and leaned back in his seat, attempting to get a grip of himself.

'Not that I can see – it all seems to be okay now. Thanks again for helping me with that.'

'It's no problem but you really should have someone take a look at the whole system.' Ben knew she was right of course: a house that size would need constant maintenance. He just hadn't made up his mind if he would be the one to do it. Was there any point in staying there now?

'Have you thought any more about decorating the room – how you'd like to do it? Or maybe you're going to start with another room first?'

'Er not really, no.'

'I suppose it's a bit daunting, knowing where to start. Especially when you have to make all the decisions by yourself –' She stopped, her face flushing a little as she continued. 'Sorry I wasn't implying anything. I just mean I know what it's like – having to do everything by yourself. I look back now and think I must have been mad taking it all on by myself.'

'Or brave?'

She tilted her head to the side, thinking. 'I hadn't thought of it like that really. Maybe a bit brave – but mostly mad I think. At first I kept thinking I needed a second opinion for everything but then I got used to it and began to trust my own judgement.'

Despite himself, Ben was intrigued and wanted to know more. 'You said you moved here with Jamie – do you have other family?'

'My mum and sister both still live in Edinburgh, which is where I grew up. My dad died soon after I left school … That wasn't an easy time.'

'You were close to him?'

She answered with a sad smile. 'Shortly after that, I went to France where Paul was working – he was a ski instructor I'd met the year before on holiday. Becoming pregnant – well, it wasn't exactly planned. We returned to Edinburgh and married and after Jamie was born we lived in the Highlands.' She paused, a shadow crossing her face. 'One day Paul had an accident off-piste and was killed. That was when I moved here with Jamie – just the two of us.'

'I can only imagine how difficult that must have been for you,' Ben said, under no illusions that Eva Harris had had her share of dark days. He watched as she seemed to compose herself with a little shake before lifting her cup and regarding him with a curious look.

'And you – do you have family in London?' Ben was aware how friendly Eva had been towards him. If he was honest, he had felt wrong-footed by her openness at first, unsure how to handle it. But very quickly he found himself becoming comfortable with it, feeling at ease in her company. He didn't exactly want to give his life story but thought the least he should do was be more upfront with her.

'No immediate family now. I lost my father too, when I was ten. I was an only child so after that it was just my mother and me. She … she died six months ago.'

'Oh, I'm so sorry.'

Ben felt grief and guilt rear their ugly heads and quickly shut them down.

'After she died, well that's when I knew I wanted to leave London. But I didn't think I'd be moving here on my own.' He ran a hand over his jaw, aware Eva had shifted in her seat and was listening intently.

'When I was offered this job at the university, it was my partner Samantha who flew up and viewed the house. I was desperate to leave London and start a new life here. We were all set to make the move.' He paused, took a breath before continuing.

'Then with a few days to go before the move she told me she'd changed her mind. She didn't want to leave London, didn't really like the idea of Scotland after all. So, I came on my own. Which is why I'm now living in a house that is ludicrously big for me,' he finished with a resigned shrug.

'That must have been terrible for you. Were you together long?' Eva asked quietly.

'Two years.'

'Quite a long time.'

'Suppose it is. Although when I look back now I can see we didn't actually spend that much time together – I'm not even sure how well we knew each other.' Ben stared into his coffee cup, thinking.

'Why do you think she changed her mind?'

'A job opportunity she couldn't refuse apparently but really I think we wanted different things. She was talking about house parties from London while I was imagining rooms with children running about. We didn't even discuss it much so I'm not sure what that tells you.' So absorbed in his own thoughts Ben was almost surprised to look up and see Eva's gaze on him, her expression understanding.

'I think I know what you mean. After Jamie was born I wanted to settle down, find a good place for him to grow up. But deep down I don't think Paul was ready. I think he was still looking for the next adventure.' There was a pause, the silence between them feeling significant in some way and although Ben found himself intrigued, wanting to know more, instinct told him they had each divulged enough for now.

'Sounds like we both arrived here in difficult circumstances,' he said simply.

Eva looked down at the table, her fingers tapping the side of her mug, appearing deep in thought. She looked up, her green eyes bright with sudden inspiration.

'Jamie and I usually make pizzas on Wednesday nights – our midweek treat. Why don't you join us this week and I could give you some ideas for your house?

I have loads of paint charts, colour swatches. And I can give you the name of a heating engineer ...' She looked at him eagerly, making it all sound so simple. A voice inside Ben's head told him he was supposed to be keeping his distance and this wasn't a good idea. But at the very same time he heard himself accept her invitation. He felt himself being drawn towards her and was powerless to stop it.

***

'Mum, how do you work out the circumference of a circle?'

'Um, not sure. Hang on, I'll need to have a look.' Eva had just finished sprinkling cheese on to home-made pizza bases and was now adding sliced tomatoes. Although she made pizzas every week tonight felt different. Knowing Ben would be joining them, she could feel herself fussing and growing nervous, her stomach doing strange little flips. She hoped inviting him had been the right thing to do. She sensed it hadn't come easily to him, revealing his mother's death and the end of his relationship. Now that she knew more about him she understood why he'd appeared so tetchy when they first met and was prepared to admit she had formed the wrong impression of him.

She had enjoyed having coffee with him. He'd been easy to talk to – in fact she was surprised how much she'd revealed to him. She brushed away her doubts, telling herself she was simply being neighbourly. He was on his own, life hadn't gone the way he had planned, and she certainly knew how that felt. She wanted to be friendly and on good terms with her new neighbour and she was genuinely interested in helping him with his house. The confusing part was finding him so attractive.

A new relationship had never entered her head since Paul – not seriously. There were fleeting moments when the idea of having someone was appealing but the reality of it was … well, scary. Meeting Paul when she was so young and then years of being on her own hadn't exactly left her brimming with confidence in that department. She kept her life simple by focusing on Jamie, the business, and nothing else.

Ben may have nudged certain feelings to the surface but Eva intended to put them straight back down again where they belonged – the risks to her and Jamie were too great. Anyway Ben had just come out of a relationship and Eva could only imagine what Samantha had been like. Probably an ambitious high-flyer, sophisticated and glamorous – basically everything she wasn't. There was no way Ben would be interested in her so why her thinking was even heading in that direction she didn't know.

She wiped her hands on a cloth and joined Jamie at the table. 'Let's have a look.' She pulled his book towards her, wishing it was English or history, anything but maths. Eva felt herself jump as the front doorbell sounded.

'I'll get it.' Jamie scampered off to answer it, any excuse to escape. Eva had explained to Jamie that Ben was coming for dinner so they could get to know their neighbour and as she suspected he was unfazed by it.

'I also said I might give him a few suggestions for decorating. Do you think that's a good idea?' she had asked him.

'Cool, you're good with all that stuff.'

Eva had felt a little glow of pride. 'You really think?'

'Yeah. It'll be good for you to have something to do.' He'd given her a sheepish grin.

'I have plenty to do thank you very much.' She had swiped him playfully.

Eva now grabbed the clasp from her hair and shook it free as she heard Ben and Jamie talking in the hall. When Ben appeared in the kitchen doorway she tried to act casual but her body instantly reacted to the sight of him. Doing her best to ignore her racing pulse, she smiled a welcome to him.

'Hi.' Eva indicated a seat at the table for him. 'Hope you're okay with a kitchen supper.'

'Compared to what I've got next door this will be fine dining.'

Eva saw his eyes flit around the room, taking it all in, and she imagined the kitchen next door without the MacKenzies' warmth and presence to be a cold and lifeless place.

'Help yourself to a drink.' Eva indicated glasses, a jug of iced water, and an opened bottle of chilled white wine.

'Unless there's anything else you'd prefer?'

'No this is great, thanks,' he replied taking a seat beside Jamie who was hunched over his jotter again, tapping a pencil against his head. 'What subject are you doing?' Ben asked him.

'Maths,' Jamie moaned. 'But I'm kinda stuck.'

'Would you like me to have a look? Maybe I can help.' Jamie willingly turned his jotter round showing Ben the offending question consisting of finding the size of angles for six triangles shown on the page.

Eva moved around the kitchen, preparing a salad and finding plates. Listening to them discussing Jamie's homework, she smiled to herself. If she was honest it was a bit of relief to have someone else to look at it. Eva's attempts at maths homework usually ended up with one of them shouting in frustration but she could hear Ben's voice now, endlessly patient. Eva began to clear a space on the table, her eyes drawn to Ben's long fingers pointing to something on the page.

'I get it now that you've explained it,' Jamie was saying. 'But I know I won't remember how to do it later. I really hate maths,' he sighed.

Ben gave him an understanding smile. 'Don't worry, you'll get the hang of it. I remember finding maths difficult especially when I started high school. Do you play chess at all?'

Jamie frowned, shaking his head. 'Donald was going to teach me but then they moved and Mum doesn't know how to play.'

Eva silently thanked her son for highlighting her inadequacy in front of Ben who was explaining to her son how learning to play chess had benefitted him at school.

'My dad taught me and it helped me with lots of things – especially problem solving and concentration.'

'So could you teach me to play chess?' Jamie's face shone with enthusiasm. Ben looked slightly taken aback for a moment, perhaps not expecting such an instant response.

'Jamie! You can't just ask like that – I'm sure Ben's too busy.' Eva threw an apologetic look to him but he seemed keen.

'No, I'd love to – I used to really enjoy playing.'

Eva smiled in appreciation at his offer, knowing anything to do with sports or games was a no-brainer as far as Jamie was concerned. With the maths homework completed, Jamie shut his jotter with a resounding thump and the conversation moved easily to football.

'What position do you play?' Ben asked.

'Usually forward: that's where I like best.'

'Yeah? So do you score many goals then?'

'A few but I'm more of a winger – I like to set 'em up.'

'I was more of a rugby man myself. I played for my university up until a few years ago, played in an amateur league and we did all right ...'

Eva sneaked a look at Ben, matching his physique to the knowledge he played rugby making perfect sense. She pulled the pizzas from the oven thinking how nice this all was. Homework done and now football talk – almost too good to be true, she mused, rolling the cutter along the pizza base and hearing a sudden warning alarm sound in her head.

She recognized a small part of her was feeling defensive, as if she had allowed Ben into her inner sanctum. And while she was happy to have him here, saw how much Jamie was enjoying it, at the same time she didn't want him getting used to something that wouldn't always be there. She told herself not to read too much into it. Jamie certainly wouldn't and they were going to be living next door to each other after all; they should all get along.

'These look great.' Ben rubbed his hands together as Eva served up. She had introduced the idea of home-made pizzas to try to get Jamie interested in cooking. He got to choose the different toppings on the proviso he helped prepare them. Tonight, he had grated the cheese and sliced the mushrooms. A satisfied silence fell as they all tucked in. It was new and strange sharing food in their kitchen with Ben whom they'd only known a matter of days. But it didn't feel wrong or uncomfortable, Eva realized. Jamie, through a mouthful of food, suddenly decided to bring up the activity weekend.

'Mum, have you made up your mind if I can go on the trip?'

'Er, not yet.' She narrowed her eyes at Jamie – not a topic she would have chosen to bring up now but had to admire her son for seizing his opportunity in front of Ben.

Eva could only watch helplessly as Jamie picked up the leaflets that had been piled to one side of the table and started to show Ben the promotional glossy photos of picture-perfect moments of children swinging from ropes or about to jump into water pools, their faces beaming.

'Okay, Jamie. I'm sure Ben's seen enough now,' Eva interjected after what felt like an interminable time, asking him to clear the table.

'That was really great, thanks,' Ben enthused. Eva was glad he appeared to really enjoy his food.

'Can I go upstairs and play on my game now?' Jamie asked once he'd finished his duties.

'Go on then but only half an hour on a school night. And can you take Hamish up with you please?' All during the meal Hamish had been sniffing about under the table, Eva gently shoving him away with her foot hoping Ben wouldn't notice. Jamie thanked Ben for helping him.

'Does that mean you can you help with my homework from now on? Mum's pretty rubbish at maths,' Jamie cheerfully told Ben as Eva's face flushed. True, she was useless at maths but that didn't mean she necessarily wanted it broadcast in front of Ben. She shuddered to think how easy he must have found Jamie's level of maths. If truth be told Eva had been struggling with Jamie's maths since the end of primary school.

'I'd be happy to help but only if that's okay with your mum?'

Eva felt Ben's eyes regard her earnestly and she experienced a wave of gratitude that he'd respected her role. 'As long as you don't mind then it's fine with me. Thanks.'

As Jamie and Hamish made their way noisily upstairs, Ben picked up the leaflets again from the outdoor activity centre at Ardentinny and read through some of the activities that Jamie had been so eager to show him. Eva must have read the leaflets a hundred times, scrutinizing every printed word. She had googled them, read reviews, and still couldn't find a single thing that indicated it would be anything other than a fantastic and safe experience for her son. Ben regarded her, one eyebrow raised.

'I take it you're not too keen?'

'Is it that obvious?'

'It sounds like fun.'

'Sure, if you like rock climbing, gorge walking, and generally endangering your life.' She knew she sounded prickly.

'I can't think of many boys his age who wouldn't,' he replied reasonably.

Eva let out a sigh. 'I know I have to let him go. It's just – I find it difficult. I get scared something terrible will happen to him if I'm not there.' The words had tumbled out before she'd even realized she had admitted her fears to Ben, leaving her feeling exposed in some way.

'I can understand.'

'You can?' she asked surprised.

'Well, obviously not as a parent. But I can remember my mum worrying about me especially after my father died. At the time it was a pain. But as you get older, you appreciate how precious that love is from a parent. I'm sure he will be okay,' he said gently, holding her gaze for a moment before Eva blinked and looked down to sweep an invisible crumb from the table.

She wasn't sure she wanted him to sound so understanding. It made her think what it would be like to have someone else, to have that other voice in her life to reassure her. It wasn't a luxury she often allowed herself. There was a small, mildly awkward pause before Ben drained his glass and spoke.

'Anyway, thanks for the pizzas. They were delicious.'

'Well thank you for helping with Jamie's homework. Are you sure you don't mind helping him? And teaching him to play chess? I hope you don't feel cajoled into anything – Jamie can get a bit carried away. I'd understand if you didn't want to or didn't have time.'

'Honestly, I don't mind at all – in fact, I'll enjoy it. Apart from my work at the university, I don't have any other commitments,' Ben told her.

Whilst reassured he seemed genuinely eager to help, Eva wondered if she should be directing the question more to herself as a warning. As lovely as it was seeing her son getting on so well with Ben, the alarm bell was ringing again, asking how wise it was letting Jamie get too close to Ben. For now, she put the worry aside.

'I'll put the kettle on. Would you like a coffee?' She stood up but Ben held up his hand.

'Please, let me make it for you.'

'Oh. Thanks. But you know what I'd really like? A cup of tea.'

'I think I can just about handle that.' After a few pointers from Eva, Ben put the kettle on and found mugs.

'This makes a nice change. Jamie's happy to help with pizza but he doesn't seem so keen to master the art of making his mum a cup of tea.'

'Sounds like a typical boy,' Ben observed with a lopsided smile.

'I guess so.'

While Ben made tea, Eva gathered the details of a heating engineer and a plumber she had put aside to give to Ben. She passed them over to him when he rejoined her at the table.

'This is the name of the heating engineer I've used and he's very reliable. The plumber – well, he knows what he's doing but just to warn you he'll arrange a time and then turn up whenever it suits him, usually two hours later.'

Ben frowned. 'Tradesmen tend to be a law unto themselves, don't they?'

Eva nodded in agreement. 'I think that's why I decided never to need a man for practical things.'

Ben was looking at her and she wasn't sure that had sounded right.

'So er, I learnt to do most things around the house for myself – decorating, plumbing, and so on. It's important for me to be as self-sufficient as possible,' she clarified, blushing slightly.

Eva took a drink, noticing Ben was holding the piece of paper she had given him loosely between his fingers, a slightly uneasy expression on his face. He shifted uncomfortably in his seat, raking a hand through his hair.

'Look, there's probably something I need to tell you.' He held her gaze for a moment and Eva felt a strange sensation spread over her skin.

'To be honest, I don't know if I'll stay in the house.' He indicated towards next door with one hand. 'It probably makes more sense to look for somewhere smaller. Maybe a flat or something ...'

'Oh.' She hadn't expected that at all. She wasn't sure why but she suddenly felt deflated. It shouldn't matter to her but the prospect of him moving just didn't sit right with her. It would be a shame, like giving up on the house in some way. And she didn't particularly like the thought of having another neighbour so soon. She was kind of getting used to this one sitting beside her. The fact he was pleasant, intelligent, attractive … they were side issues. She thought about his situation and supposed she could understand why he might want to move.

Eva took a sip of her tea, casting her mind back to a couple of winters ago. A December afternoon, Jamie and Fraser had settled down to watch a *Home Alone* film while Eva had given Heather a preview of one of the bedrooms she had recently finished decorating. Clutching a rather large glass of wine, Heather had been so impressed she'd asked Eva if she would decorate her dining room, which – after the rampages of three children – was looking more shabby than chic.

Eva assumed it had been the wine talking but the next day Heather assured her she'd been serious. And so every morning after dropping Jamie at school, Eva had turned up at Heather's house armed with her tools until a week later she revealed a stylish new dining room her friend had been delighted with.

After that, Heather had asked her to decorate her mother's living room. Eva bit her lip, feeling suddenly nervous. An idea was forming in her mind, but she hesitated before saying it out loud.

'Look, this might sound crazy and I'm not sure how you'd feel about it. But I could do it for you. Decorate your front room I mean. Whatever happens, whether you sell or not, it's probably a good idea to have it done anyway. She stole a quick glance at Ben but was unable to read his expression so she carried on regardless.

'Obviously I'm not a professional but I know I could do a good job. I've decorated all my own rooms and I've done a few jobs for friends as well ...' Eva stopped. In her own head, it had sounded a reasonable idea but the way his dark eyes were fixed on her now ... What had she been thinking? Oh God, she'd made a total idiot of herself and she flushed with embarrassment.

'Actually you know forget it; it's a silly idea.' She laughed weakly.

Ben regarded her thoughtfully, running a hand round the back of his neck.

'Is it something you'd really want to do?' he asked doubtfully.

'Honestly? Yes. I've kind of run out of things to do in my house. I enjoy running my business but interior design and decorating is something I'm really passionate about – I'd love to do more of it in fact. I guess it gives me a sense of fulfilment the guest house doesn't. Plus I like to keep busy.'

A smile touched his lips. 'I'm beginning to see that.' He paused and Eva felt his dark gaze settle on her. 'So what would it involve exactly?'

'Well, I'd have to strip off all the wallpaper, prepare the walls for painting. I think the window frames need some attention and obviously the ceiling has to be fixed –'

Ben was frowning. 'I'm not comfortable with the idea of you climbing ladders or doing anything risky – I wouldn't want you harming yourself.'

97

'I'm used to it and I'm fully up-to-date with health and safety procedures, so you don't need to worry.' Eva smiled in reassurance but couldn't deny there was something nice about his concern.

'And you'd manage to do it all on your own?'

'Sure. I'd really only need help shifting the furniture out of the way if you could give me a hand with that –'

'Sounds like the least I could do.'

'So … does that mean you're happy for me to do it?'

'As you say, it's probably a good idea to have the work done whatever I decide to do with the house.' He took a deep breath, letting it out slowly and with an imperceptible shake of his head smiled at Eva. 'As long as you're happy to do it … then yes, that would work for me.'

Eva felt a small rush of pleasure that he'd agreed. 'Really?'

'Why not?' He shrugged, smiling at her. 'But I'll pay you of course.'

Eva shook her head emphatically. 'You can pay for the materials but my time is free.'

'Are you sure?' He frowned at her.

There was no way she would take money from him but equally she didn't want him to be uncomfortable with the arrangement. 'As long as you're happy to help Jamie with his maths now and again then that's more than enough payment.' Eva held her breath, hoping she hadn't overstepped some boundary. But to her relief Ben seemed happy with that and nodded.

'I guess we have a deal then.'

'I guess we do.' She smiled back. 'So when would you like me to start?'

He shrugged. 'I'll give you back the keys and as far as I'm concerned you can come and go as you please.'

'I'll probably just come in after Jamie's left for school and I've walked Hamish. Does that sound all right with you?'

Eva finished her tea, her head already busy with things to organize. She loved that moment of starting a new project. Although Ben had admitted to being pretty clueless with interiors she couldn't assume she had a total free rein.

'Are there any colours that are a definite no-no? Anything you really dislike or are you happy to leave it up to me?'

He narrowed his eyes, pretended to think hard. 'No lime green or pink,' he said solemnly.

'Okay, I'll try and remember that.' Eva laughed. 'And what about the flooring? Will you want a new carpet or maybe you'd like to have the floorboards sanded? It wouldn't take much ...'

She stopped. Ben was holding up his hands, looking bemused. She took a breath. 'Sorry, I tend to get a rush of ideas ... I'll let you know when I need any decisions made.'

'Really, I wouldn't know where to start choosing colours and ... things. I'm happy to leave it all in your hands.'

'If you're sure then.'

'I'm sure. And Eva?'

'Yes?'

'Thanks.'

After Ben had left, Eva finished off tidying up the kitchen, feeling a buzz of anticipation. She ignored the voice in the back of her head asking why she was really doing this and whether it was such a good idea. She hoped she hadn't made a monumental mistake. But then she chided herself. It wasn't such a big deal; it was just a mutually beneficial arrangement between neighbours. She thought of the long winter months ahead. It would be good to have something to occupy her.

Chapter Six

Eva was running. Faster and faster she ran but her legs were about to buckle from under her. Desperately she tried to escape but something dark and menacing was closing in behind her, so close it was almost touching her.

She jerked awake drenched in sweat, her body trembling with fear. She sat up, her heart pounding so strongly in her chest she could hardly take a breath. It was always the same horrible dream – the one she'd first had after Paul was killed. Months could go by but Eva always knew the dream was the first sign anxiety had come knocking.

Rubbing her face, she checked the time to discover it was only five o'clock. Knowing there was no chance of sleep again she climbed out of bed, wrapped herself in her dressing gown, and went down to the kitchen. Her breathing still felt raggedy and her fingers fumbled as she filled the kettle. She glanced at Hamish still curled up in his basket – too early even for him.

Resisting her usual caffeine fix she opted instead for a soothing camomile tea and carried her cup through to the living room. She opened the blinds and took a seat opposite the window. Taking slow deep breaths she let the darkness and silence wash over her until she began to feel her heartbeat return to normal – a ritual she'd done many times before.

Eva could pinpoint the exact moment anxiety became part of her life. It had been the moment she opened her front door in the small cottage she and Paul rented near Aviemore to find two police officers on the doorstep. She knew by their sympathetic, sombre expressions it wasn't going to be good news. Paul had been in an accident and had been taken to hospital. With her heart pounding and stomach churning, Eva lifted Jamie from his bed and bundled him into the back of the police car. Even before they arrived at the hospital in Inverness, Eva was able to guess what had happened.

Paul had often described to her the joys of skiing off-piste. He said there was no sensation on earth to match the freedom of floating down a remote mountainside on fresh powder. He'd always tried to convince her he was safe, telling her he was avalanche aware and that he had all the right safety equipment. He even quoted statistics – skiing had proportionately fewer fatalities than cycling or swimming.

After Jamie was born, Eva had made Paul promise not to go off-piste but she knew he hadn't been able to resist. He'd been with a friend who had managed to call for help but it was too late. By the time they reached the hospital, Paul had died from a head injury after falling and probably hitting a hidden rock. Eva had no chance to see him one last time. All that life, all that energy wiped out in an instant. That night, something deep inside her had shifted – a cold fear had crept in and never really left.

Although life had moved on, anxiety had stayed as an unwelcome guest. Eva could always feel it, like a cold hand on her shoulder, ready to squeeze fear into her at any moment, a terrible legacy from that day. Since then, Eva had done everything possible to keep life stable and safe for her and Jamie. She knew that had led to her being overprotective, trying to control too much. She didn't want the unexpected or unknown in her life and yet in the last few days she felt something changing.

And Eva knew it was because of Ben. He was making her feel different, as if she was stepping out of a shell she had created. She thought about Jamie's trip and knew she couldn't put her decision off any longer. Of course she wanted him to go and have an amazing time. As uneasy as it made her feel, she knew she had to try not to give in to her fears. It wasn't fair on Jamie. Had Ben's words made a difference? Did knowing he was now next door make her feel more secure in some way? She wasn't sure.

What she did know was that life was changing and something deep within her was shifting. Jamie was growing up and she knew she had to try and embrace the change. Eva sat for a long time and finally she felt a sense of calm. Outside she could see the light beginning to reclaim the day. She took a final deep breath and knew it was time to tell Jamie he could go.

***

Ben's tutorial on thermal physics had just ended and he was back in his office sitting at his desk. It was Friday afternoon and outside darkness was looming so he switched on his small desk lamp for extra light. His office at the university was a tiny, cramped room at the end of a long corridor in the physics building. There was a small window overlooking the quadrangle and just enough room for a desk, a chair, and a bookshelf. Ben loved it.

Slowly he could start to feel his life in London fade away. Almost as if he was recovering from living in the city, from the constant barrage of sights and sounds that had assaulted his senses every day. He thought about his old life – on and off the tube, the crowds and fumes and the gruelling hours. He had been a cog in a never-ending wheel of money-making madness and he was relieved he was no longer part of it.

Now he could breathe again, think again. He felt himself slipping back into the life he'd once known but had given up. He was beginning to find his feet again – running workshops and tutorials, preparing lectures – it all came back to him.

As he felt his old life begin to ebb away, so he began to feel more settled here and that included thinking about Eva Harris. It was slightly unnerving how easily thoughts of her seemed to flow into his mind and invade his thinking. Opening up to her in the past few days and revealing so much about himself had felt alien to him at first. When he arrived here, his plan had been to concentrate on work and keep contact with people to a minimum.

But as soon as he was in her presence something changed; he felt a different person.

He had pondered if the arrangement with Eva to decorate his house was a wise one, but not for long. He knew there was no way he was going to turn down her offer. There was something appealing about the idea of her being around. Just the thought of her in his house made it feel warmer somehow, as if she was breathing new life into it. He told himself he shouldn't overthink it. She was being friendly and helpful – that was all. Although he hadn't expected her offer, it didn't totally surprise him either.

She had an energy and openness about her that he found compelling. She had genuinely sounded keen to do the work and she clearly knew exactly what she was doing. Plus it would give him time to decide what to do. Whatever his plans for the house it wouldn't do any harm to have the front room decorated. He had enjoyed sitting and sharing pizza and helping Jamie with his homework far more than he cared to admit. Jamie seemed a great kid, polite and friendly, and he was genuinely looking forward to helping him again and, of course, teaching him to play chess.

He had no doubt Eva was an amazing mother – that much was obvious and he admired her strength for coping the way she did. He had no intentions of intruding where he wasn't wanted or needed but he wondered if she missed having someone, if she still grieved for her husband, still longed for him. She had suggested that they had wanted different things but that didn't mean they hadn't been committed to each other and nothing could take away the bond of having a child together.

Eva had come round a couple of days ago and he'd helped her shift the furniture from the front room into the hall where she'd thrown dust sheets over everything. He'd given her back the spare keys and they'd agreed she would come and go when Jamie was at school. This morning he'd noticed she had made a start stripping the wallpaper but he was leaving her to it, not wanting her to think he was checking up on her.

Managing to drag his thoughts away from Eva he unlocked his drawer and pulled out a pile of essays for marking. He took the first essay from the top and read the first sentence when a knock at the door interrupted him.

'Hi, Ben.'

Ben looked up and silently cursed when he saw Kat Morgan. A newly minted PhD graduate, she was working under the direction of Professor Drummond and had just started a two-year post to gain experience planning research projects and managing students. Ben was all for ambition, but hers came with a pushiness he had no time for.

Ben suspected her casual clothes were in fact precisely calculated for maximum effect – her top just low enough to reveal a hint of cleavage, the jeans tight enough to leave little to the imagination. Her dark hair fell below her shoulders and her face was a mask of heavy make-up. When he'd first been introduced to her she had smiled, her handshake lingering that little bit too long. His first instinct had been to keep his distance and nothing had changed that, except all these unannounced visits to his office were making that difficult to do. She closed the door behind her and strolled over, perching herself on the corner of his desk.

'How're you doing?' she asked coyly as Ben automatically moved back in his seat.

'Um, good thanks.'

'It's almost five o'clock on Friday, Ben. What are you still doing at your desk?'

He patted the pile of essays in front of him. 'Just about to start some marking,' he told her.

'A few of us going for drinks – fancy joining us?'

Ben shook his head apologetically. 'Not tonight thanks. I'm going to stay on for a bit and then get home.'

'I'll let you off this time.' She pouted her lips in an exaggerated manner and twisted a coil of hair round her finger. 'But you haven't forgotten the seminar next week? Remember I'm collecting you.'

Damn, he'd forgotten he'd agreed to that. Professor Drummond had asked Ben to attend a two-day seminar at Glasgow University. Kat had cornered him a few days ago, suggesting she pick him up, and Ben hadn't been quick enough to come up with an excuse. He'd been busy at the time and had tried to think of some way to extract himself from the situation but failed miserably.

'Er, sure. I'll see you then,' he muttered. She looked at him expectantly.

'I'll need your address silly, won't I?' Reluctantly he gave his address, just happy to have her leave his office but not before she gave a coquettish little wave. Ben grimaced and turned his attention back to his marking.

After a few fruitless minutes Ben knew his concentration had been broken and realizing he was hungry decided to head back to his house. He could make something to eat and carry on with his marking there. He packed up and started the walk home, the peace and quiet of St Andrews still a welcome novelty.

Just as he turned a corner he saw Jamie ahead of him, sauntering along seemingly in a world of his own. He was laden down with bags, his jacket and a racquet, which clattered to the ground just as Ben caught up with him. He reached down to pick it up, smiling up at Jamie.

'Hello, Jamie.'

'Hi, Ben!' The boy grinned back and Ben thought he looked happy to have company.

'I can carry this for you. You look a bit weighed down. Are you heading home?'

'Thanks. We were playing football and one of the boys hurt his leg so we waited for his mum to come and collect him and then she decided he needed to go to the hospital so I'm, like, really late. Mum's gonna be mad with me.'

Ben smiled to himself. He hadn't exactly been hurrying. 'Does she know you're on your way home now?'

'Er, no.'

'Why don't you give her a quick call – I know you'll be home in a few minutes but it'll be good for her to know. Always best to keep your mum happy, eh?' He winked conspiratorially.

Ben remembered that age, a tricky time. Hormones, girls, schoolwork ... lots of changes to cope with. Like Jamie he'd lost his father and he knew how it felt to be an only child. He recalled his own mother worrying about him and with no siblings, being her sole focus could be overpowering at times. Only when he was older did he realize how special it was to have that unconditional love. With the call made, they continued on their way.

'Do you have a game of football tomorrow?' Ben asked.

'Yeah,' Jamie sighed heavily.

'You don't sound too happy about it – are you up against a difficult team?'

'Nah, we'll beat them no bother. It's after the game. Some of the boys are going to the cinema to see the new *Star Wars* film but I can't go 'cos I promised Mum I'd go to a training class with Hamish.'

'Ah well, you need to keep your promise then. I'm sure you'll get to see the film another time,' Ben consoled but had to admit he could understand some of the boy's angst at having to miss what had been his favourite films at his age.

'Suppose,' Jamie murmured not sounding too convinced.

'Have you seen the original *Star Wars* films?' Ben asked. 'Think the first one was late 1970s – they were a different class.'

'Uh-uh, don't think so.'

They turned into their street, Ben noticing the stark contrast between the two houses waiting for them. His house lay in darkness while light glowed from the other. Eva had come to the door now, her eyes seeking out her son and then shifting to Ben. Jamie had been chatting continuously and carried on as they reached Eva.

'My friend Fraser's big brother is at the university and he said they've got a great sports bit. He said you can do almost any sport you want – American football, judo, and everything. Do you get to do all that if you want?' He looked up at Ben earnestly.

'I guess so, yes.'

'I'd love to try all those things,' Jamie exclaimed eagerly.

'Well, I know the university runs sport taster days. Maybe I can take you and your friend along to the next one so you can try a few things?'

Jamie's face lit up. 'Really? That'd be awesome!'

Ben hoped he hadn't overstepped a mark but noticed Eva rolling her eyes jokingly in exasperation at her son before ushering him into the warm house.

'Think you've just made someone's day.' She laughed.

'Well, I keep meaning to investigate the sports department and haven't got round to it so I guess this way I'll have to go.'

A delicious aroma of cooking infused the air between them and for a moment he imagined eating with Eva and Jamie again before pulling himself together. They looked at each other for what felt like a long moment and Ben realized he needed to say something.

'I should …'

'Would you …'

'Sorry you go first,' Eva said.

He discarded the image of a shared meal, tightening his grip on the bag containing his students' essays – that was the reality of his evening. 'I've got a pile of marking – I should really get home,' he said.

'Oh, of course,' Eva replied. 'And thank you.' She took the racquet from Ben's hands and they shared a smile before Ben turned to go back to his house.

Chapter Seven

Eva pulled off her rubber gloves and stretched out her back. Finally, she had removed all the wallpaper. She had spent the past two days in a cloud of steam, stripping off layers of wallpaper that had been up so long it had flaked away in little pieces and fallen at her feet in a sticky mess. But now at last it was all off and the room looked much bigger and brighter.

She glugged a mouthful of water from her bottle and then, after a short break, set about lifting the carpet. Donning her heavy work gloves she used her knife and started to cut the carpet into manageable strips before rolling them up. Who needed the gym she thought hurling bits of carpet into a corner of the room. Eva was pleasantly surprised to discover the wooden floorboards were in good condition. It wouldn't take too much effort to restore them to their original glory – some sanding and varnish and they would look lovely.

Much later, covered in sweat and with aching muscles, Eva surveyed the room. Apart from a bit of plastering where the leak had caused damage, the room was ready for decorating. She had created a blank canvas to work with and, most importantly, it no longer felt like the MacKenzies' room. It felt a little sad, as though Eva was stripping away their memories, but she knew they'd had a happy life here and now it was someone else's turn. Would that person be Ben? she pondered.

Knowing she was working in Ben's house – doing it all for him – felt personal, made her feel connected to him, but as she gazed around the room now, it dawned on Eva she had no real plan what to do next. Usually her mind was brimming with ideas and colour schemes. She'd always found it easy decorating her own home but with a sinking feeling realized all her creative thoughts seem to have floated off somewhere else.

As if looking for inspiration she wandered into the hall where boxes remained unopened, a clear sign that Ben hadn't made up his mind about staying, and Eva felt her heart drop. Feeling horribly nosy but unable to stop herself, she walked through to the kitchen. She wasn't sure what she was looking for but wanted to see if she could get more of a feel for Ben's life that might give her clues for decorating.

As in her own house the kitchen was a large, bright space but there was nothing to suggest Ben was cooking or even spending much time here. Some fruit – not too fresh-looking – and an opened packet of biscuits lay on the worktop and several dirty mugs competed for space with a stack of books on the table. In one way she supposed it was typical for a man living on his own but there was also something sad – an emptiness – like seeing a life on hold.

She couldn't see any personal touches or anything to show he intended to stay and certainly no hints of his personality that might help with her decorating. She thought about what she did know about him. She knew he had experienced loss and that his relationship had ended. She had detected a serious, studious side to him but also a very human side. She had observed how good he was with her son.

Watching him and Jamie walking home the other night and chatting so naturally she had felt her heart do a little dance in her chest. Jamie responding so positively to Ben was lovely but she hoped she wasn't making a mistake allowing her son to form a bond with him. She had missed the MacKenzies dreadfully at the beginning but the truth was she was beginning to get used to Ben as her new neighbour.

Thinking about him now Eva felt the stirrings of something. She couldn't identify the exact feeling – part fear, part exhilaration. She was beginning to realize how much it mattered to her that Ben liked what she created. Whatever her motives had been when she first offered to do the job, it was beginning to feel about much more than paint and wallpaper, almost as if she was investing part of herself into the project. The sudden knowledge that she didn't want him to leave struck her with her a force that left her feeling bewildered and she bolted out of the kitchen as if she'd been caught trespassing.

With forced concentration she focused on tidying up: folding up the stepladders, packing away her tools, and tucking all thoughts of Ben neatly to the back of her mind. It had been a long day and her early start was finally catching up with her. This morning she had told Jamie he could go on the trip. Remembering the expression on his face made her smile. Breaking his own no-hugging rule, he had voluntarily wrapped his arms around her.

'Thanks, Mum! I love you.'

'I love you too,' she had replied, holding him tightly.

***

The aroma of freshly brewed coffee met Eva as she walked into The Coffee Hut on Saturday morning. Heather was already settled at their usual table and waved over to her. Eva shrugged off her jacket and flopped down beside her, grateful for the seat.

It had been a bit of a disastrous Saturday morning with the discovery that Hamish had chewed one of Jamie's new football boots. When they had finally hunted down his old pair, it was only to find they had no laces and somehow it was all Eva's fault. Heather nodded in sympathy as Eva recounted the morning's events.

'I don't know how you did it three times. I can hardly manage with one.' Eva shook her head in dismay. 'Please tell me it gets easier.'

Heather let out a little puff of air. 'I wish. They seem to go from happy to snappy in the blink of an eye, don't they?'

'Jamie refused to take any responsibility whatsoever. No matter what I said, all I got were eye-rolls and smart comebacks,' Eva said indignantly.

'Ah yes, I know it well. Arguing with kids is a losing battle believe me, I have the scars to prove it.'

'The days of Play-Doh and jigsaws seem a lot simpler now,' Eva sighed despondently. This morning Jamie had seemed to resent her very being, making her feel like the most annoying human on the planet. Heather tried to reassure Eva and make her feel better.

'This is an awkward age; they're just figuring out who they are. There's a lot more outside influences now. But don't worry, it's all perfectly normal.'

'I certainly hope so,' Eva muttered. 'I wasn't even sure football would be on with all this rain.'

'There was a pitch inspection earlier and the referee decided to go ahead. They're lucky to get their game though; the forecast isn't looking good.'

'You see, that's why I love you. You know everything.' Eva grinned at her friend.

'Only the stuff that matters to mothers who have a vested interest in having their sons run around for ninety minutes.'

Eva chuckled. 'That's true. Jamie's definitely a happier boy after a game of football even if the weather is terrible.'

'Playing football in Scotland's not for the faint-hearted that's for sure.' Heather put her mug down, raising her eyebrows at Eva. 'So?'

'So?' repeated Eva innocently.

'Who was he?'

Eva rolled her eyes. She hadn't seen Heather since the morning she'd driven past her standing with Ben and had known she'd never escape the inevitable inquisition.

'My new neighbour, Ben Matthews. He's working at the university, a physics lecturer.'

'Really?' Heather contemplated this information for a moment before taking a bite of a warm croissant. 'Bit rugged for a physics lecturer, isn't he?'

'Um, he does seem quite well built I suppose,' Eva said lightly.

Heather put her cup down with a clatter, sudden comprehension dawning on her features.

'Ah, so he's the new hottie Professor!'

'He's the what?' Eva chortled.

'I heard Adam mention it. You know how he's studying engineering at the university – well, his friend Amber is doing chemistry and she told him apparently a new Professor in the science faculty has caused quite a stir among the females. Bet his classes are popular then!' Heather sat back, looking quite pleased with this turn of events. 'What's he like?' she asked Eva, her voice full of interest.

'Well, he wasn't the easiest person to talk to, at least not at the beginning. But I've got to know him a bit better and when he came round for pizza –'

'He came round for pizza?' Heather exclaimed.

'Don't get excited. I was just being neighbourly.'

'So what did you find out about him then?'

'Um, he's from London. He seems kind of quiet and recently split with his partner.'

Heather's eyes lit up. 'He's got a broken heart? That's even better.'

'How do you work that out?'

'You can console him of course.'

Despite herself Eva laughed, shaking her head. 'How many times have I told you – I'm not on the lookout for a man. I'm happy the way things are.' Eva had said the same thing to Heather countless times. She had Jamie and her business and that was enough; she didn't need anything else. There were times she looked at her friends or other mums in the playground and envied their lives full of children, and husbands or partners. But that wasn't the way her life had unfolded and there was no point in wishing for something that wasn't going to happen.

'Anyway, I'm not going to console him – at least not the way you'd like. But I am going to decorate his living room!'

'Oh wow, that's great –'

'What's great?' Freya had bustled over carrying a tray laden with coffee cups and cakes. 'Jack's taking over for a bit so I can come for a natter.' Freya cosied up on the sofa as she often did on a Saturday morning when Heather and Eva came in.

'Thanks,' Eva said, taking a mouthful of lemon drizzle cake and rolling her eyes to the heavens. 'Delicious.'

Heather happily filled Freya in. 'Eva's going to be decorating her new neighbour's front room who just happens to be a hunky physicist.'

'Is that the guy you had coffee with in here the other day?' Freya asked innocently.

'You had coffee with him as well?' Heather's eyes almost popped out of her head.

'He was very handsome – had that whole smouldering thing going on.' Freya made a dreamy face at Heather.

'Some people might think he's handsome,' Eva said primly.

'And you don't?'

'Technically he is, yes … I suppose …' Eva lifted her coffee to hide her blush although she didn't mind her friends' gentle teasing. Being married and having Jamie so young she always felt she'd missed out on a chunk of growing up. She had gone from what was essentially her first big romance to becoming a wife, mother, and then widow. Men were just something that happened to other women – boyfriends, husbands, partners – they simply hadn't been on her radar.

'So you're decorating his house?' Freya broke into her musings.

'I offered to decorate his front room. He had a leak in his living room –' Eva ignored Heather snorting into her coffee '– which I helped him with, so it left some damage. We got talking and I found myself offering to decorate the whole room,' Eva finished matter-of-factly.

'You are pretty handy with a paintbrush – I can vouch for that.' Heather's head bobbed up and down.

'So how's it going then?' Freya wanted to know.

'That's the thing. For some reason I'm struggling with ideas, almost like I've got a mental block.'

'You're usually so good with decorating.'

'I know,' Eva sighed. 'I've haven't used one before, but I was thinking of creating a mood board.'

Heather's eyebrows shot up suggestively. 'A what board?'

'It's an arrangement of colours, material scraps, images – anything to help give ideas,' Freya explained before turning to Eva. 'You've never had trouble before. Do you think you might be trying a bit too hard?'

Eva felt her shoulders slump. 'Could be a possibility,' she admitted.

'Hold on, I might have something to help you.' Freya bustled away. Eva and Heather exchanged mystified glances while finishing their coffee. A few moments later Freya reappeared with a small canvas.

'Before I start painting a seascape I work on a small canvas first. It helps to give me an idea of colour and composition.'

Eva studied the canvas, which she realized was basically layers of colours representing a view of the beach. The sky was painted light blue while the hills in the distance were shown with strokes of white. The rocks in the foreground were brown and the water turquoise. Light grey depicted the small peaks of foam in the water and finally there was a sweep of golden beige for the sand.

'I adore the colours in this; it's really lovely,' Eva said appreciatively.

'Do you think it might help you at all?' Freya asked.

'You know, I think it just might,' Eva replied thoughtfully. Even though it was quite abstract, the layers of colours captured the essence of the sea, sand, and sky and Eva could already feel it igniting ideas, imagining Ben's brown leather sofas set against very pale grey walls.

Heather nudged Eva, reminding her it was time to go and watch the last part of the football game. Neither of them was overly keen at the prospect of leaving the warmth of the coffee shop for the cold sidelines of the pitch but duty called. Full of cake and clutching Freya's canvas, Eva pulled on her jacket, feeling much happier.

Chapter Eight

The following Tuesday Eva let herself into Ben's house. She had arranged for the plasterer to come and fix the ceiling where the leak had been and finally she felt as if her creative juices were flowing again. Freya's canvas was propped up on the mantelpiece and Eva now had a clear picture in her head of how the room would look. She was determined to detach any feeling she may have for Ben and do a professional job.

Eva hummed to herself, feeling a light-heartedness she hadn't felt for a long time. The morning was bright and light filtered into the room. The walls were dotted here and there with small patches of paint where Eva was testing an assortment of samples. She was leaving them to dry so she could see how they would look at different times of the day.

Having decided to restore them to their former glory, today Eva was going to tackle the floorboards and she'd hired a floor sander, which stood in the corner ready to go. Wearing her usual dungarees, she tied her hair in a ponytail in readiness to start work. On her hands and knees, she was using a pair of pliers to pull out some leftover carpet staples still intact in the floor when a sound made her freeze. She listened to a movement coming from upstairs and realized someone was there. Her heart rate rocketed as she heard footsteps making their way down the stairs.

From her position on all fours she saw his feet first. Eva slowly raised her head to find Ben looking at her from the doorway. He was smiling at her, his eyes soft and amused.

'You all right there?'

Eva rocked back on her heels, her hand on her chest. 'God, you gave me a fright – I didn't realize you were in the house.'

'Sorry, I didn't mean to startle you.' He strolled over to Eva, holding out his hand to help her up. She took his hand, feeling his warm, strong fingers wrapped around her own, and knew there was little chance of her heart rate recovering. Visibly fresh from a shower, his hair was still damp and he wore a snug-fitting white T-shirt and blue joggers. He was close enough for her to breathe in the citrus fragrance of his aftershave and she blinked hard, trying to dispel the image of him in a hot shower.

'I'm going to a seminar at Glasgow University later so I'm working from home this morning,' he explained – not sounding overly keen. Instead he seemed more interested in looking round the room. 'So, how are you getting on in here?'

'As you can see I've lifted the carpet and all the wallpaper is off – I think I lost count after four layers of wallpaper. The plasterer is coming to do the ceiling later; in fact he'll be here soon.'

'Plastering not one of your many skills?' he teased.

She smiled back. 'Not brave enough to try. It's quite a difficult skill to master and I'd be scared to make a mess of it,' she admitted, looking up at the ceiling with her hands on her hips. Ben strolled over to her, his closeness not exactly helping her attempts to be detached and professional.

'I pretty much know what I'm going to do now but actually now that you're here, I was wondering if you had any ornaments or pictures that you wanted me to use in the room?'

'Um, I don't think so.' Ben rubbed the back of his head. 'There might be something through here.' Eva followed him into the hall where he looked at the pile of boxes before he appeared to gather the energy to start shifting them about. Eva watched the muscles of his arms flexing as he lifted a particular box and placed it in front of her, looking at her with a half-smile.

'I don't really have many er, ornaments but you might find something in here. I packed a few bits and pieces.'

'You don't mind if I look through this?'

'Not at all but I don't think you'll find anything. I really didn't have much to bring.'

Eva tried and failed to picture the life he had left behind. Her own house was full of small mementos, ornaments, and keepsakes that she liked to see every day.

'I'm just about to make a coffee. Would you like one?' He nodded towards the kitchen.

'Sure, thanks.'

While Ben set about making their drinks Eva ambled through to the dining room, which Ben was clearly using as a makeshift office. The table was covered in papers and books. She glanced at the sheets of paper filled with calculations and indecipherable scrawls. She picked up a paper lying on top, her eyes drawn to the heading – *Causal Probabilities in Quantum Field Theory.* Wow. Not only did Eva find it impressive and intimidating that Ben understood that; she also found something slightly intoxicating about it.

Ben appeared at her side and handed her a mug. 'That's the seminar this afternoon,' he said casually nodding to the paper.

Eva tried to think of an intelligent question but failed miserably. 'Causal probabilities ... so what's that exactly?'

'The question of causality asks whether or not your theory respects the laws of special relativity – the laws of space and time. If your theory isn't causal then you could have all sorts of weird things happening, one event affecting another before light has had the chance to propagate between them ... In the movies it's called time travel.' He glanced at her and smiled lopsidedly. 'Sorry. I can get a bit carried away.'

Eva shook her head, putting the paper back down. 'That's all right, I'm afraid it's just not something I can easily get my head around. But it does make me feel slightly inadequate.'

'Are you kidding? You should never feel inadequate,' he said forcefully. 'You run your own business, bring up your son. And look at all your practical skills – you know about heating systems, plumbing, decorating – I reckon that's pretty impressive.'

She regarded him over the rim of her mug. 'You don't look like a scientist, or at least how I imagine one to look.'

'And how would that be?' He returned her gaze, his eyes glittering.

'I don't know. A cloud of mad white hair, a crumpled lab coat, glasses.'

'I can wear glasses if you like.' The look he gave her sent a flash of heat up and down the length of her body and she struggled to make her voice sound normal.

'So um, how did you get into physics?'

'I suppose it was my dad really. He used to take me to the Natural History Museum in London when I was very young. One time there was this exhibition about the moon landing and I just remember something inside me come alive, you know. Something really caught my imagination. And I was lucky I had a good physics teacher at school who really encouraged me.'

Eva remembered how patient Ben had been with Jamie with his maths homework and thought he must be a good teacher. It must be nerve-racking to stand up in front of a classroom of students but presumably he was used to it.

'So where did you teach before St Andrews?'

He didn't answer immediately. Instead he moved to the table and Eva saw his shoulders tensing as he

126

gathered papers. 'I haven't taught for the past five years. I've been working in the City as a financial analyst.'

Eva frowned, not understanding. 'Do you mean you were a banker?'

He nodded. Like everyone, Eva had heard the stories about big money and city trading. Weren't they ruthless and greedy? She'd registered his expensive car in the driveway, and the quality of his few pieces of furniture was unmistakable but apart from that there had been nothing showy or ostentatious about him that she could see. Eva had simply assumed he had always been a physics teacher.

'So, why did you get into banking?'

'The same reason anyone does. Money,' he replied dryly.

Eva closed her eyes briefly, memories of her father flitting into her mind. He'd always looked so worn out, working such long hours and for what? They were able to live in a lovely house, have holidays, and buy nice things. But Eva was convinced it was the relentless pressures of work that caused his heart attack, and she would have traded any of the material things for him to still be alive. Affording nice things in life was fine but not at any cost. Eva tried to live by and instil in Jamie a sense of values not based on money.

Up until now, she'd thought of Ben as a scientist, a teacher. She liked that he was clever, could apply his mind to higher matters and let's face it, she found his intelligence incredibly sexy. Knowing he'd been a City trader surprised her and not in a good way.

'So um, what exactly did you do?'

'I worked for an investment bank,' he sighed.

'What did that involve?'

He gave a wry smile, before answering. 'On a good day working fourteen hours ... on a bad day, longer.'

'And you enjoyed that?' Eva didn't intend her tone to sound so harsh and judgemental but it was too late; the mood had shifted and she saw Ben's expression change. He looked at her, a nerve twitching in his jaw, and she felt herself flinch under his gaze. Eva didn't know whether to be thankful or not when she heard loud rapping at the front door.

'Oh, that'll be Gary. I'll get it'

'Fine. I should go and get ready,' he said, turning to go.

'Of course, sorry. I didn't mean to hold you up.'

Eva opened the door to find Gary on the doorstep looking his usual cheery self.

'Hi, Eva.'

Wearing overalls and carrying the tools of his trade, Gary was one of Jamie's football coaches at the weekend but a plasterer by trade. He had been recommended to Eva when she'd first moved into her house. They chatted for a few minutes as Gary set himself up and started to mix the plaster. Eva watched as he handled the plaster using his trowel and hawk. He worked rhythmically and quickly, making it look easy as he used broad strokes to cover the surface of the ceiling.

Eva suddenly felt miserable, not sure what had passed between her and Ben just now but certain she had antagonized him in some way. She shouldn't have shown her distaste for his job in the City. Who was she to pass judgement – it had nothing to do with her. But she couldn't deny it, discovering he had worked in the City she felt a stab of disappointment. She gave herself a shake and picked up the bucket to fill with hot water from the kitchen so she could start to give the floor a clean.

As she passed through the hall, the doorbell rang and with Ben upstairs, Eva decided to answer it. She swung the door open to a young woman. Slim, heavily made-up, and with the shiniest hair she'd ever seen. Eva's eyes darted to her bright red nails wrapped around a bottle of champagne. Clearly not expecting Eva to answer the door, her posed smile fell for a second before she recovered.

'Hi, I'm here for Ben?'

'He's –' Eva started to speak but the woman didn't wait; instead she barged in past Eva just as Ben appeared at the bottom of the stairs. He had changed into navy trousers and a white shirt and looked so painfully handsome Eva wanted to cry. He glanced uneasily at Eva and then at his guest. Eva felt herself shrink. Never before had she felt self-conscious in her dungarees. They were comfortable; they were practical. But she looked like a workman she thought miserably. She hadn't even washed her hair today.

'Hello, Kat. You're early.' Ben's tone was cool and Eva bit her lip, sensing their earlier conversation must have really irritated him.

'Hi, Ben. I thought you might want to show me round your new house before we go. You didn't tell me it was so big!' She looked around and turned to Eva and briefly looked her up and down. 'And you have decorators in – how lovely.'

Ben looked awkwardly over at Eva. 'Actually, this is –' He started to speak but his visitor gave him no chance to finish and instead put a proprietary hand on his arm.

'A little housewarming.' She waved the bottle and turned to Eva giving her a condescending smile. 'Would you mind putting this in the fridge?'

'I can take it –' Ben reached out to take it but Eva was too quick.

'Of course,' she said through gritted teeth. She marched into the kitchen, yanked open the fridge, and shoved the bottle on the bottom shelf as she heard the woman's voice drift through from the hall.

'Did you have a chance to read over the notes I sent you? I highlighted the parts I thought you might want to discuss, in particular the argument that quantum mechanics in not locally causal ...'

Eva loitered at the kitchen sink, making a pretence of washing her hands. So she was one of Ben's colleagues. And not just one with shiny hair but one with a brain to match Ben's.

'We'd better get going. The traffic might be heavy.' Eva heard Ben, his voice sounding terse as she dried her hands. The front door closed and unable to help herself, Eva scurried through to the living room to sneak a look out of the window just in time to see a red sports car pull away. Eva felt herself slump. Ben hadn't even come to say goodbye, clearly eager to be off.

What had just happened? Everything seemed to be going well and then they'd had that strange conversation about his work and now he had zoomed off with his colleague. Eva was beginning to think of Ben as a friend, someone she could talk to. She wondered if she'd been forcing herself on him in some way. Her hand flew to her mouth with a sickly realization that it had all been her – her asking him for coffee, to share pizza ... even offering to decorate his house. Was he just being polite all this time? She thought they were becoming friends, even imagining a chemistry between them but seeing him with his colleague she knew they belonged in different worlds.

She cringed thinking she'd actually asked him what the conference was about. Eva pictured them discussing quantum theory or whatever the hell it was before it became so heated they jumped into bed together for a night of physics-fuelled passion. Eva was more likely to be the person who came to change the sheets in the morning. With a heavy heart she turned from the window, the thought of them together making her feel quite nauseous. She gave herself a little shake when Gary spoke to her.

'All right, Eva? That's me about finished.' Gary smiled, oblivious to her turmoil. Eva squared her shoulders and returned his smile.

'Thanks, Gary. How about a cup of tea?' she asked. Gary grinned his approval and Eva went to fill the kettle.

***

Rattled by his conversation with Eva, Ben stared despondently out of the car window as Kat drove them to Glasgow. Kat was chatting, something about an amazing hotel she'd stayed at in Milan last year, but Ben wasn't really listening. He was thinking of Eva's reaction when he'd told her he worked in the City. It was like seeing a reflection of his own distaste for what he had done. Hearing the hint of scorn in her voice and seeing the dismay in her face bothered him.

He remembered his first big bonus; it was crazy. He had stared at his bank balance, hardly believing the amount of zeros. Every day he had worked in the City was a day his mother received the best care but that didn't stop him questioning his decision every day and it didn't stop him feeling guilty.

Ben rolled down the window in the car slightly to let in some air. The strong scent of Kat's perfume and the way she kept turning her head to speak to him was making him feel claustrophobic. He wasn't oblivious to the obvious charms his colleague was now displaying. She wasn't exactly subtle about it. They just did nothing for him; in fact they left him cold. He cast her a sideways glance, realizing something about her reminded him of Samantha. The type of woman who knew what she wanted and wasn't afraid to go after it.

Ben had never had trouble attracting women and although he wasn't a saint, he'd never felt the need to chase after women the way some of his friends had done when they were younger. He'd had relationships but nothing that had lasted or been serious. Studying, working, and caring for his mother had been his priorities and somewhere along the line between losing his father and then his mother to her illness, he supposed he had instinctively put up defences as a means of self-preservation.

He had met Samantha in the club he frequented some evenings after work, people from different offices often blending into one crowd as the night wore on including his colleagues and the group Samantha was with. Ben had noticed her – she always looked good and dressed impeccably – and occasionally they acknowledged each other with a nod or a smile.

One evening she had dropped her purse, Ben picked it up for her, and they had started talking, ordering more drinks. He wasn't sure who asked who but they had arranged to meet for brunch and a walk on Hampstead Heath the next day. They had talked easily, Ben liking that she was direct and undemanding, and they started to see each other regularly or at least as often as their schedules allowed.

Samantha always had that polished look and Ben had been aware of the admiring glances when she walked into a room. She exuded confidence and always knew the right things to say to the right people. They ate in the best restaurants, got their hands on the impossible-to-get tickets for the theatre, and received endless invitations to dinner parties. She talked about her work. A lot. Whereas Ben wanted to forget about work at the end of each day, Samantha would happily dissect her day, her colleagues, her chances of promotion.

Now with distance and time between him and his old life, Ben could see with the money he earned he'd also bought into a certain way of life. Samantha and the lifestyle were a by-product of the money he earned and he had gone along with it. He had functioned, done what he had to do. It was only after his mother died he admitted to himself just how unhappy he'd become.

Samantha had never come with Ben to visit his mother on Sunday, preferring to go to the gym and meet her friends to hang out at one of their trendy eating places. Ben hadn't minded – she worked hard all week and he certainly didn't expect her to accompany him each weekend.

But over time, as the visits grew more difficult and Ben watched his mother deteriorate, something within him began to change. He was painfully aware that when he lost his mother he would have no family, nothing to stay in London for except Samantha. A vision of the future began to form in his mind. He dreamed of leaving his job in the city, returning to academia, and starting a family. The dream had sustained him on the darkest days and made the visits more bearable.

The day of his mother's funeral was the worst of his life. Rain fell from black clouds as he thanked friends and the care workers from the care home who had attended. But of course there had been no family to share his grief and Ben had felt a terrible darkness in his heart.

It had been his birthday the following week and to his dismay Samantha had produced tickets for a day at the races for them. 'Something to cheer you up,' she told him. The idea of going was bad enough; that she had misread his mood so badly was even worse.

Even so, when he told her about being in touch with Professor Drummond and the idea of starting afresh in Scotland she had initially been all in favour. Now he knew the move for Samantha had been about her career. Her dream had been about setting up a business and when a better offer came along, she had simply taken it.

He inhaled deeply, staring out of the car window, reminding himself that was all behind him, all in the past. They had come off the motorway now and the traffic had started to slow as they made their way to the university through Glasgow's west end. Kat tapped her manicured nails on the steering wheel and Ben smiled to himself. She was impatient to get wherever it was she was going. An image of Eva's hands came to his mind. They didn't looked manicured; they looked hard-working and natural.

'So, I take it you're going to the ceilidh?' Kat broke into his reflections.

He nodded. 'I don't think we have much choice in the matter. Hasn't the Professor issued a three-line whip?'

'Sounds like fun – we can go together if you'd like?'

He would go for the Professor, of course, but the thought of the evening wasn't holding much appeal for Ben at the moment. He wasn't exactly feeling sociable.

Kat looked at him expectantly when he didn't respond immediately. For some reason thoughts of Eva filled his head again and the words left his mouth before he'd thought it through.

'Thanks, but actually I'm already bringing someone.'

'Oh?' Kat threw him a cool look. 'Well, I guess I'll need to find someone else then.'

Chapter Nine

'Ta-dah!'

With a flourish, Eva revealed the cake she had made for Fraser's twelfth birthday party. Heather looked in admiration at Eva's butter icing creation, complete with glitter sugar and chocolate sprinkles.

'Wow, that looks great, thanks.' She beamed at her friend gratefully. Eva placed it on the table in Heather's dining room already groaning with sandwiches, sausage rolls, biscuits, and bowls of sweets.

'Are you sure you'll manage with all these boys in your house?' Eva asked as Jamie took off in the direction of what sounded like general mayhem.

'Are you kidding? I wouldn't know what to do with myself if I didn't have a house full of testosterone. Plus I have my secret weapon.' She peeked open a cupboard door, pointed to a bottle of Merlot, and shut it again. Heather's husband Douglas emerged from the kitchen holding a giant helium balloon, emblazoned with Happy 12th Birthday, and greeted Eva with a peck on the cheek.

'It's too late for me but you should escape while you can,' he implored Eva before Heather shooed him away.

'Honestly, I can stay and help if you want.' Eva giggled.

'Nope, I've got it all covered. Food, films, and sleepover although I doubt much sleeping will get done.'

'Sounds perfect.'

'What about you? What will you do?'

'All sorted. I also have a bottle of wine and I'm sure there's an episode of *Friends* I haven't seen fifty times yet.'

'Really? Nothing else you'd rather do?'

'Like?'

'A gorgeous woman like you, a night of freedom. The possibilities are endless ...'

Eva rolled her eyes at her friend.

'Okay, I know. But you will be all right won't you?' Heather asked with genuine concern, fully aware how nervous Eva was being separated from her son.

'Don't worry about me, I'll be all right,' Eva reassured her.

'And Jamie will be too. I promise I'll look after him.'

'I know you will.'

'Anyway, have you not seen the forecast?' she said tipping crisps into a bowl. 'A storm warning has been issued for the east coast. You'd better get going.'

Eva made her way back to her car, a little shiver running down her spine as she looked up at the sky, which had grown ominously dark. The drive home was a nightmare. Within minutes of leaving Heather's house the rain had started and was lashing against the windscreen and bouncing off the road. Gripping the steering wheel she negotiated the massive puddles that had sprung out of nowhere, vaguely listening to a voice on the radio explaining the weather system responsible for the storm and predicting worse to come.

Relieved when she finally reached home, Eva slammed the front door gratefully behind her. She spent the rest of the afternoon securing everything outside and making sure the chicken coop was safe. Hamish ran around manically, refusing to leave the garden, and looked up at Eva accusingly. 'They'll be fine,' she reassured him.

In her living room Eva lit the log burner and poured herself a glass of wine, determined to try and relax despite the wind howling down the chimney and buffeting the windows. She'd be fine tonight on her own, she told herself, but deep down she wasn't looking forward to it. She knew other mums who would relish having a night to themselves but it filled Eva with dread.

Suddenly, the lights flickered on and off. Poor Heather. She could imagine the boys at the sleepover were probably hyper by now. She took several large sips of wine as she flicked through the channels deciding what to watch. The remote almost flew out her hand when Hamish, with some canine instinct for impending doom, let out an almighty whine at the precise moment the room plunged into darkness. Only a small light given out by the fire remained; other than that everything was black.

Eva froze for a moment wondering what to do. Surely it would only take a few moments to restore power? Carefully she made her way over to the window to look outside but couldn't see a single light from anywhere. The sky was suddenly illuminated by a flash of light and Eva quickly turned from the window and gathered Hamish up as the inevitable roll of thunder followed.

Remembering the supply of candles she kept in the hall cupboard, she went in search of them. She felt her way along the wall using the light from her phone, Hamish following behind her. Eva's heart hammered in her chest as she fumbled her way around, finding candles and matches and lighting as many as she could. She took another mouthful of wine, telling herself not to be ridiculous. Every bone in her body seemed to jump when she heard knocking at the door. She picked up Hamish again and held him close as the wind and rain rushed in through the open the door.

Ben stood there and the sight of him almost made Eva weep. Whether from relief that he wasn't a crazed psychopath or that his solid, muscular form filled the doorway she didn't know. He spoke but the roar of the wind made it impossible to hear properly. She gestured for him to come in and quickly closed the door behind him, leaning her back against it. In the hallway he seemed huge, the darkness somehow enhancing his presence.

'Are you okay?' he asked.

'Yes,' she replied, surprised to hear the shakiness in her own voice.

'Where's Jamie?'

'He's at a sleepover.' The thought that he might be here to check on them was as unsettling as it was unexpected. She really didn't want to sit through this storm alone and the several swigs of wine she had consumed gave her enough courage to ask him to stay. 'Would you like to come in for a while?' Eva braced herself for a polite decline but to her relief he smiled.

'It's not a night for being alone,' he replied.

The last time she'd seen Ben he was being whisked away by his colleague and since then Eva had distracted herself by pouring all her energy into sanding and varnishing the floorboards. She felt slightly foolish now for thinking there might be something between them. Seeing him with his colleague and discovering he'd been a City trader, she realized she didn't have him figured out at all. Finding him so attractive – what woman wouldn't after all – and easy to talk to didn't amount to really knowing him.

Eva led the way into the front room and realized she may have gone slightly overboard with the candles, the flickering lights suddenly looking more like the setting for a romantic seduction than one for making polite conversation with your neighbour. Eva watched Ben's dark silhouette make its way to the sofa.

Depositing Hamish back down on the floor she asked Ben if he'd like a glass of wine.

'Sure, thanks,' he said.

Feeling more accustomed to the dark, Eva brought another glass from the sideboard and sat down beside Ben. She poured him a glass and topped up her own just as another gust of wind shook the window, prompting a pathetic cry from Hamish. Ignoring her normal no-dog-on-sofa rule, she allowed him to jump up between them, thankful for the small canine barrier between her and Ben. Hamish nuzzled closer to Ben, clearly happy to relinquish his role as alpha male.

'Was it Jamie who wanted a dog?' Ben asked chattily.

Eva nodded. 'He kept asking and I kept resisting because of the business. But eventually I gave in. I'm not sure if Jamie chose Hamish or Hamish chose Jamie, but it was love at first sight. So now Hamish is part of our family – and totally useless in an emergency as he has proved tonight.'

'Well I'm here now, Hamish, so you're off the hook.' He ruffled Hamish's fur, his words making Eva feel all warm inside for some reason. She reached for her glass thinking she should probably slow down just as her phone pinged. Grabbing it, she scanned a message from Heather.

'My friend Heather, letting me know Jamie is fine,' she told Ben. 'She's managed to get through on her mobile to the power company – apparently they're working on restoring the power but it could take a while.' Eva tapped out a reply saying she was okay, stifling a giggle imagining Heather's reaction if she could see her now sitting in the dark with wine, candles, and Ben.

There was a pause and Eva suddenly felt awkward, unsure what to say. It bothered Eva how their last conversation had ended, like a black cloud hanging between them. She tried to picture him as a City trader but just couldn't do it – something didn't sit right about it. But she certainly hadn't meant to sound so disparaging. She glanced over at him now, rubbing Hamish's ear.

Maybe it was the darkness, but she felt acutely aware of how close he was to her and her senses seemed to be in overdrive. She really wished she didn't notice the way the candlelight danced across his features, casting a shadow over his cheekbones and illuminating his dark eyes. Maybe it was the wine and she hoped she wouldn't regret bringing up the topic again but suddenly she needed to apologize.

'You know, when you told me you worked in the City, I – I didn't mean to sound judgemental. I'm sorry.' There was silence and Eva realized she was holding her breath.

'You don't need to apologize. Working as a trader wasn't something I ever wanted to do.' His words filled Eva with relief for some reason and her shoulders loosened.

'So ... why did you do it?'

She heard him exhale in the darkness. 'It's a long story.'

'I'd like to know it,' she said quietly. 'If you don't mind telling me.'

He appeared to contemplate his glass for a moment before slowly setting it down on the table and starting to speak.

'After I finished my PhD at Oxford I got a job working at the university – teaching and research, which I loved. I'd go home to see my mum as often as I could. She still lived in the house where I grew up near London. She was living a happy active life, working part-time in a local bookshop, seeing friends.' He paused for a moment before continuing.

'I began to notice small changes in her but nothing I could put my finger on exactly. When she started to forget things I assumed it was because she was just getting older. But she started to do a few strange things – asking odd questions, losing things, and becoming confused. I had this horrible instinct something wasn't right. We went to the doctor and that was the start of a whole series of testing.' He sighed, a deep heart-wrenching sound that made Eva want to reach out and touch him.

'Eventually she was diagnosed with early onset Alzheimer's.'

'Oh, Ben, I'm so sorry.'

'After that, things deteriorated quickly. They put her on various medications, which helped with the confusion but over the next year things became more difficult. I was worried she'd have an accident – she would leave the water on, wander off on her own. I went home as often as I could during the week, even staying the night and leaving early in the morning to get to work.'

'That must have been terrible.' Eva blinked, filled with sadness for him.

'At first I thought about giving up work to look after her but because her immune system was so weak she kept getting infections. It became clear she needed proper medical, intensive, and round-the-clock care. I did a load of research and found a specialist care unit reasonably close to where she lived. It was as non-institutionalized as I could find and she'd get the best care. But of course it came at a cost. There was no way my salary at the university would cover it.' He rolled his shoulders and took a breath.

'One day I happened to meet an old friend from university who worked in finance. We got chatting and I couldn't believe how much he was earning. He told me the big financial firms were always on the lookout for analytical thinkers and that he could set me up with an interview.' He paused again and Eva knew this wasn't easy for him.

'So, that's what I did – I left the university and took a job at an investment bank. It meant I could pay for my mother to receive the care she needed. She lived there for five years until she died. It would have broken her heart if she'd known I'd turned my back on my university career but seeing her suffer more than she had to would have been worse.'

They sat in silence for a few moments, Eva's heart aching for him, and she placed a hand on his arm.

'Ben, I'm so sorry for what you've been through. And I'm sorry for reacting the way I did but now I know why you did it I totally understand. You had a difficult decision to make but you did what you had to so your mother was in the best possible place. Your decision was based on love – anyone can see that.' Eva lifted her hand from Ben's arm, instantly missing the warm solid feel of it.

'And now you're back working at a university – your mum would be happy about that,' she said softly.

'Yeah, she would.' Eva was relieved to see the briefest of smiles pass over his lips.

A contemplative silence settled over them and Eva sensed Ben seemed more relaxed as he leaned forward, taking the bottle to top up their drinks. He passed Eva her glass and their fingers brushed together, the feel of his skin sending a prickle of heat through her.

'Jamie told me he's going on his trip.' Jamie had taken homework to Ben's house a couple of times and the arrangement seemed to be working well.

'To say he's excited is an understatement.'

'But you'll still worry about him.' It wasn't a question.

'I guess that's what happens when you're an only parent – you end up doing the worrying for two.'

'You must miss Jamie's father?' Ben spoke gently.

'I do at times. But mostly I feel sad for Jamie not having his dad and for Paul dying so young.'

'I'm sure he would be very proud of you both.'

'Thanks,' Eva said. 'We're doing all right now but when we first arrived it was a different story. I was daunted by what I'd taken on and it didn't help that my mum took every opportunity to point out she thought I'd made a huge mistake. I think what she really wanted was for me and Jamie to go back to Edinburgh so that she could look after us.'

'But you didn't want to?'

'I know my mum wants the best for me, but let's just say our ideas of what that might be are very different. The most important thing for me was to be self-sufficient. My dream was to run a business that let me be with Jamie and provide a stable life for him.'

'And the chickens, the dog, are part of that dream?' His voice was gently teasing.

'Safety in numbers I always think.' She laughed. Tilting her head to the side, she looked at him. 'What about you – being here, is that your dream?'

His gaze locked on hers and Eva felt as though some invisible force was inching their bodies closer together. He looked at her mouth then back to her eyes, and Eva moved towards him, the desire to touch him overwhelming. And then, like a spell suddenly broken, the lights came back on.

***

His dream? Right here, right now felt like a dream, thought Ben, thankful the lights had saved him from answering. He watched Eva blink as her eyes adjusted to the light. He was sitting tantalizingly close to her, close enough to see the flecks in her green eyes. Curled up on the sofa, he could see she was wearing jeans and a white embroidered top. A simple silver necklace nestled on her collarbone. She looked sleepy and her hair was slightly tousled, a heady mix of vulnerable and sexy. She smiled shyly at him before she unfolded her legs and stretched out her body. She rose from the sofa and went over to the window, Ben watching her every move.

'The street lights are back on too,' she told him. Ben forced his gaze from her and surveyed the room. They had been sitting on one of two chunky sofas, scattered with coloured cushions. A low, dark wooden coffee table sat on a wool rug in front of a cast-iron fireplace and in one corner a shelved recess held books and photo frames. Everywhere he looked there was warmth, colour, and texture.

'Wow. What a great room.'

'Thanks.' She looked directly at him, a teasing challenge in her eyes. 'So you trust me to do a good job in your room?'

'Implicitly,' he replied solemnly, hand on his chest.

'Good. Have you taken a sneaky look at your room – it's almost finished.'

'Not recently. Think I'll wait for the grand reveal.'

'Okay then, I'll let you know when that'll be.' She gave a small laugh and he loved the sound of it.

Ben knew it was time for him to go but thoughts of the ceilidh entered his head and he knew it was now or never if he was going to ask Eva.

'Actually, there's something I wanted to ask you – a favour.' He hesitated and she smiled at him expectantly. 'The Professor in our department has organized a ceilidh for St Andrew's Day – next Friday. It's for charity and, well, I'm never really comfortable with these work things and wondered if you'd come with me? I know it's a bit short notice ...'

He saw Eva blink in surprise. 'Me? Why would you ask me?'

'Well, why wouldn't I?'

She frowned, giving her head a little shake. 'I can think of a few reasons. That's the weekend Jamie's away. I don't have anything to wear ...' She seemed to be talking more to herself but then her gaze shifted to Ben, her eyes narrowing slightly.

'Are you sure there's not someone else you'd rather go with?'

'No.'

'Not someone from the university?'

'No,' he replied, puzzled.

'You're sure?'

'Is there something I'm missing here?'

'I just thought you might want to take your colleague – you know, the one with shiny hair who came to your house?'

Ben frowned before realizing who she meant and then burst out laughing. 'Kat? God, no.'

'Really? I thought you two ...'

He lifted an eyebrow. 'Yes?'

'I'm not sure – that you'd have lots to talk about.'

'You and I have lots to talk about, don't we?'

'But not science-y things.'

He managed to keep a straight face as he replied. 'That suits me just fine.'

'Well, if you're sure.'

'I'm sure. She's a colleague, that's all. I'm happy to show support for her academic aspirations but let's just say I don't want to encourage any other aspirations she may have.'

'And they won't think you've brought your decorator?'

'I highly doubt it and even if they did, so what?'

Eva was smiling at him now. 'In that case yes, I'd be happy to come with you.'

He gave his head a small shake, thinking how she was unlike any woman he'd ever met and the prospect of spending time with her sent a surge of anticipation through him, a feeling he hadn't experienced in a long time. Ben started to make a move to leave, his body feeling strangely reluctant. 'I guess I better go,' he said.

'Um, right. Thanks for coming round, to check we were all right.'

'You'll be okay?'

'Of course. I have Hamish to look after me.'

Ben's instinct was to stay; he didn't want to leave her on her own. He wanted to make sure she was safe but like a physical force, he felt a much more primal instinct and decided that staying probably wasn't a good idea. They made their way through the hall and Ben stopped before he opened the door, their eyes meeting. He lifted his hand and tenderly brushed his finger against her cheek.

'Goodnight, Eva.'

Ben left Eva's home and heard the fading rumbles of the storm, his body racked with all sorts of tensions. He doubted he'd get much sleep tonight.

Chapter Ten

It was Friday morning and Eva was trying desperately to hold herself together, determined not to embarrass Jamie. Knowing she could quite easily dissolve into a pool of tears, she dug her nails into her palms, hardly believing her son was going away without her.

Last night she and Jamie had packed his bag. Eva had ironed name tags onto his jumpers, trousers, and towels and then stuffed them into his rucksack with the hundred pairs of socks he'd been told to bring. She tried to go along with Jamie's obvious enthusiasm but seeing him so excited reminded Eva so much of Paul.

She had blocked the image of Paul getting ready to go off skiing, the glint in his eye he used to get at the thought of the adrenaline rush to come, which used to terrify her. This was different she told herself, taking a deep breath and speaking in the calmest voice she could find. 'Listen carefully to all the instructions, okay? And do exactly what you're told.' Eva looked Jamie in the eye, willing him to keep safe.

'Yeah all right, Mum. We've been over this like ten times,' he said with a sigh.

Sometimes Eva looked at her son and was amazed at how grown up and tall he was becoming but today all she could see was her little boy. The boy she had cherished since the moment he was born and who was now standing with his rucksack attached to his back ready to leave her. Heather came over and gave her arm a reassuring squeeze.

'You know, worrying is an occupational hazard but you do tend to take it to extremes. He will be all right, I promise.' She smiled.

'I know,' Eva sighed, wishing she could be so relaxed. The bus pulled up outside the football club and the babble of voices grew louder as the children who had been standing in groups with parents now started to make their way towards the bus. A coach with a clipboard ticked their names off. Hugs and final kisses were given. Eva quickly wrapped her arms around Jamie.

'Have an amazing time. I love you!' Eva waved as the bus trundled out of sight, feeling as if her whole world was disappearing.

'I had a feeling you might need one of these,' Heather said, handing her a tissue.

'Thanks.' Eva sniffed with a weak smile and proceeded to blow her nose.

But there the sympathy ended. Heather was not giving her chance to wallow. She had already informed Eva that she was taking charge after the boys left and, knowing this was the night of the Professor's ceilidh, had organized some pampering.

'Honestly, Heather, you don't have to do this,' Eva pleaded. Going home and burying herself under

152

a blanket for the next forty-eight hours suddenly sounded very appealing. Heather treated her to a withering look.

'When did you last do anything just for yourself?'

'I, um –'

'Exactly. You deserve a day with some pampering. What else would you do now? You'd go home and just obsess about Jamie staying safe.'

Unable to deny it, Eva sighed. 'But I don't want to make a big deal about tonight. It's just a casual invitation.'

'Well then, you're going to look casually sexy.'

Eva knew there was no point in protesting, not when Heather had that sparkle in her eye – she was a woman on a mission and there was no stopping her. She'd have to try and go with it even though her mind and body were sending mixed signals about what she wanted from tonight.

Eva hadn't expected Ben to ask her to this ceilidh and wasn't sure what, if anything, to read into it. A favour he had called it. He saw her as a friend and you asked a friend to do you a favour. But the night of the storm kept replaying in her mind. During their conversation she had felt a real connection and then just before the lights turned back on she had felt an intensity – almost a physical heat – between them. Even thinking of it now sent tingles through her body, as if parts of her that had been frozen for years were beginning to thaw and on a massive scale.

Heather was talking to herself, looking at her watch. 'We have time for a spray tan if you want? Don't suppose you've ever had one before?'

'No and I don't want one today, thank you.'

Heather peered at her, narrowing her eyes. 'I suppose you can get away with it. You're lucky to have such lovely colouring. In that case we'll have a quick coffee before your facial. Then the hairdresser's and a bit of shopping.'

'But I don't need –' Eva's voice trailed off as Heather put up her hand.

'It's all booked now so it's too late.'

Two hours later Eva lay with her head back in a head-massage-induced trance. The *heavenly head* treatment came complimentary with her haircut and it was exquisite. It was only thoughts of the evening ahead, which kept popping into her head, that prevented her from becoming totally comatose.

Once Heather was happy everything on her list had been attended to, they drove back to Eva's house. While Heather sorted through various shopping bags, Eva couldn't resist a small smile at her reflection in the mirror. She'd almost forgotten the power of a good cut and blow-dry.

'I'm not sure what you were planning on wearing, but I have something to show you before you decide,' Heather said while Eva was busy turning her head from side to side admiring the way her hair bounced over her shoulders. She should probably be ashamed how bedraggled it had become but her appearance simply hadn't been much of a priority recently.

Heather was now pulling a slip of dark blue material from a bag and carefully unfolding it to reveal a beautiful dress. 'Wow, that's lovely,' Eva exclaimed.

'I'm glad you like it because it's for you to wear tonight.'

'I can't take this!'

'Of course you can. I bought it and never wore it. I'm two pregnancies away from ever fitting into that dress. Try it on at least.'

'All right then, just for you,' Eva conceded giving her friend a fond look.

Eva changed clothes, gently pulling the dress over her head. It had been so long since she'd worn anything pretty she almost didn't recognize her own reflection. The dress had a mesh neckline with embroidered detailing and a fitted bodice that flared out at the hips, stopping just before her knees.

'Oh, that's gorgeous. It'll be perfect for spinning round the dance floor and showing off your legs. It's fun and flirty but retains a certain elegance.' Heather's head bobbed in approval.

'Are you sure?' Eva asked, seeking reassurance.

'It's perfect. Just think of me as your fairy godmother.'

Eva shot her a comical look and curtsied. She had to confess to feeling great in it.

'I've got to say, it's good to see you in something so feminine – you look lovely.'

'Not exactly my dungarees is it?' Eva grinned at Heather.

'As hot as they are, this is even hotter, trust me.'

'What's that for?' Eva asked as Heather now handed her a glass filled with sparkling wine.

'Liquid courage.'

'Thanks,' she replied as they clinked glasses. 'But I won't need it. Nothing is going to happen.'

'Oh, I wish it was me going out,' Heather sighed wistfully. 'Talking to people, making eye contact, a little flirting, lingering looks ... Oh I forgot the excitement of a date.'

'It's not a date! And anyway, you have Douglas. You wouldn't change anything would you?' Eva looked at her friend thinking how the spark between Heather and Douglas was still obvious.

'No of course I wouldn't. It's just that feeling at the beginning. Butterflies in your stomach, a racing heart, counting the minutes until you see him again ...'

'Uh-huh,' Eva muttered, all those things sounding disturbingly familiar.

'It's really quite magical,' Heather reminisced happily, drinking more wine.

'Did you always know Douglas was the one?'

'Suppose I did. We met in a nightclub, fancied each other and that was it really – sounds quite old-fashioned now.'

'Apparently one in five relationships now start online.'

'Really? How'd you know that?'

Feeling caught out, Eva stuttered, 'I, er was just looking, you know ... at dating sites.'

Heather's head swivelled around. 'Why were you doing that?'

Eva's shoulders slumped. 'All right, I admit it. I have been having thoughts ... feelings if you will, about Ben.'

'I knew it! Oh this is so exciting.'

'I'm so out of the whole dating thing, I only wanted to know what kind of questions they asked. See if I could work out if we were compatible, if our personalities matched.'

'So what questions did they ask?' Heather sounded interested.

'Well, you had to choose words to describe yourself – like shy, affectionate, outgoing, intelligent. Then tick things you like doing – cinema, theatre, reading, shopping, dining, and so on.'

'And?'

'From the little I know about him, I'd say we have nothing in common.'

Heather chuckled, shaking her head. 'Nonsense – you two are made for each other, I can just tell.'

'How much of that wine have you had? Think about it. He reads science journals; I read trashy magazines. He's probably a member of Mensa and I have trouble finishing the easy crossword.'

'I wouldn't pay too much attention to all that stuff. It's all about the chemistry,' Heather professed, selecting various jars and tubes, which she had laid out on the table. 'It's time to do your make-up.'

'All right but I don't want to wear too much,' Eva protested taking the foundation from Heather. She applied some eye shadow, a little eye liner, mascara, and finished with a touch of pink lipstick. 'There. Will I do?' she turned to ask Heather.

'My work here is done.' Heather grinned.

Later, when they discovered Heather had managed to drink almost the whole bottle of wine by herself,

Douglas was called upon to take her home. After they'd gone, Eva was left on her own waiting for Ben to arrive, feeling madly nervous. She kept checking her phone for no reason.

She almost jumped out of her skin when the doorbell sounded and she made her way to the door on wobbly legs. She almost gasped at how breathtakingly handsome Ben looked. His hair had been neatly swept back and he wore a pale blue shirt under a smart jacket with black jeans. She saw his eyes skim over her before he smiled.

'Wow,' he said in a low voice. 'You look lovely.'

'Thanks,' she replied, snatching her coat and bag and trying to breathe normally. She closed the front door behind her, reminding herself this wasn't a date even though it was the closest she'd come to one in a very long time. The evening was cool but pleasant for walking and they strolled a short distance before coming to a little pub on the corner. Its windows glowed invitingly with light and they seemed to have the same idea.

'Do you fancy a quick drink?'

'Just what I was thinking.' Eva smiled.

The pub was busy with the sound of lively chat and had an end-of-week feel to it. Eva made her way to a small table she had spotted in the corner and took a seat while Ben went to the bar. Looking round Eva noticed how relaxed everyone seemed but she felt distinctly jittery. It wasn't just being out on a Friday night but being with a man, almost as if she was in someone else's body.

Eva certainly wasn't in the habit of eyeing up men in pubs, but as her eyes settled on Ben standing at the bar ordering their drinks she realized that's exactly what she was doing now. It wasn't just that he was tall and handsome – that much was obvious. There was something else about him, a quality that drew her to him and made her conscious of his every move. Eva sat up with a jolt as it dawned on her she was lusting after Ben. She glanced to a group of men standing at the bar. All perfectly healthy-looking male specimens ... nope, nothing. Her gaze slid back to Ben and there it was again, her body pulsing with desire.

Feeling a little light-headed she grabbed the drink when Ben placed it in front of her and gulped a mouthful too fast. Ben looked at her with concern as she spluttered.

'You all right?'

'Fine,' she replied with a little cough.

'So did Jamie set off this morning?' Ben asked raising his beer to his mouth.

Eva nodded. 'The boys weren't allowed to take mobile phones – part of the ethos of the trip. But the group leader sent a text letting us know they'd arrived safely and were settling in.'

'And how are you coping?'

'Okay so far – I'm trying not to think about it too much, keeping my mind on other things.' In fact, she should probably be thanking Ben for the first-class job he was doing distracting her. The sound of sudden loud laughter made their heads turn to a rowdy group sitting near them.

'So, is this place a regular of yours?' Ben asked with a small smile.

'Hardly.' Eva chuckled thinking of her social life. 'I don't go out that much. I actually consider parents' evening at Jamie's school a major event in my social diary.'

Ben gave a little laugh and Eva adored the way his eyes crinkled at the edges.

'My friend Heather likes to drag me to various places now and again. She thinks I should go out more, try and meet someone ...' Eva blushed, not sure why she had said that.

'And have you – ever gone out and met someone?'

'Nope.' She paused, aware she was about to admit something she'd never said out loud before. 'I suppose I haven't wanted to risk being hurt.' She lifted her eyes to find Ben watching her, with an expression she couldn't read.

'Any man who hurt you would have to be an idiot,' he said simply.

Eva picked up her glass, not sure how to respond although her insides were close to melting. She let out an awkward little laugh, trying to sound normal.

'What about you? This must be quite different after the bright lights of London.'

He looked around. 'Yeah, this is very different but nice. I like it.'

'Did you go out much – socializing?'

He rubbed a hand across his jaw. 'Working in finance in the City you kind of had to. It was almost part of the culture. The company where I worked, most of us were members of a private club. Plush and pricey – not somewhere I ever felt comfortable but after finishing a long manic day it was difficult just to go home and switch off. It was easier to go and unwind, talk shop.' He shook his head at the memory. 'That was where I met Samantha.'

'Did she work for the same company as you?'

'No, she worked in IT for another company. We kept meeting there with the same crowd after work and eventually just wound up together.'

'Doesn't sound very romantic.'

'Romantic?' The observation seemed to surprise him and he rubbed a hand around his neck before looking at her. 'No, I don't suppose it was. What you had with Paul, was that romantic?'

'More exciting than romantic I think, at least at the beginning.' Losing Paul had left her shocked, scared, and even angry at times but over the years Eva had come to terms with what had happened between them. She had difficulty imagining them as a couple today. 'When I think of him now, it's as someone I used to love but more as a friend. Obviously we had Jamie but in all honesty, I'm not sure we would have stayed together. He wasn't my grand passion.'

She sipped her drink, slightly shocked to hear herself admit that out loud but for some reason felt better for having said it. 'What about you?' she continued. 'You don't miss London and – everything?'

She watched Ben lift his glass to his mouth and slowly put it back down, his eyes never leaving hers.

'Not a single bit of it.' The air seemed to hang thickly between them and Eva felt her cheeks grow hot. She straightened in her seat, casually flicking her hair over her shoulders in a bid to appear normal, wondering if Ben was feeling it too.

'So from private clubs to ceilidhs … this is going to be quite a change for you. Have you ever even been to a ceilidh before?' she asked lightly.

'Once at university and that was a long time ago so I'd better warn you now, I won't have a clue how to do any of the dances. I take it you've been to a few before?'

'Loads. We were taught all the dances at school so they kind of stay with you for life after that. Don't worry, I'll keep you right.'

'I'll hold you to that. Here's to a good night.' They brought their glasses together.

***

Ben was having trouble keeping his eyes off Eva. He'd been pretty much mesmerized by her since the moment he'd seen her tonight. After their drink in the pub, they had made the short walk to the university. They had passed through the leafy quadrangle and entered the grand hall, which was ablaze with light and colour. The panelled walls were lined with saltire flags and hundreds of fairy lights trailed along the stained-glass windows.

The ceilidh was already in full swing and Ben had led the way to one of the tables encircling the dance floor where he spotted some colleagues. After a few introductions they had soon found themselves joining in, Ben discovering it was impossible not to be swept away by the sheer energy of the dancing. He was totally bewildered at first as he tried to keep up, finding it chaotic until he started to see the patterns and formations emerging for each dance.

Eva had helped him, trying to guide him through the steps but quite often she'd ended up in fits of giggles. She looked beautiful as she had thrown her head back laughing at his attempts. And among the noise and movement all Ben could see was Eva, his eyes drawn to her like a magnet. Watching her body move and the way her dress clung to her curves was driving him to distraction.

The Canadian barn dance had just finished and the band announced a break so people returned to their tables, grateful for a seat and refreshments. Now Eva was sitting beside him at their table, slightly breathless and her cheeks flushed.

'Are you having fun?' she asked with a grin.

He nodded. 'I am, but I'm not sure I'm a worthy partner.'

'You're doing all right for an Englishman,' she teased.

'You seem to be enjoying yourself?' he asked, loving that she looked so happy and relaxed.

'I am.' She beamed back at him. 'I forgot what good fun a ceilidh is.'

Out the corner of his eye Ben had seen Professor Drummond making his way round the tables and saw him now approach their table. Ben smiled at how distinguished and dazzling he looked in full Highland regalia.

'Ben! Good to see you.' He shook hands with Ben, his eyes already on Eva. 'And who is this lovely young lady?'

'Professor, this is Eva. Eva, this is Professor Drummond.'

In a theatrical gesture the Professor bent down to kiss her hand. 'Lovely to meet you, Eva. Don't you two make quite the handsome couple,' he said with a mischievous glint in his eye. Knowing the Professor well, Ben threw him a warning smile.

'Nice to meet you,' Eva replied.

'Did you know Ben was my best ever student? He left me for a while but I always knew he'd come back.' The Professor patted Ben on the back, looking at him affectionately. 'Now, I have to go and make speeches and thank people for their donations.' He clasped Ben's hand in two of his, shaking it. 'You especially, Ben.'

He turned his attention back to Eva, giving her a wink. 'He's a wee bittie special but I think you might know that already.'

As the Professor wandered off to the next table Kat suddenly appeared, clinging on to Dan, one of the research assistants who fortunately didn't look too unhappy about it.

'Hi, Ben,' she cooed.

Sensing Eva bristle, Ben instinctively rested his hand on her waist, pulling her towards him. 'Eva, these are my colleagues: Kat and Dan.'

Kat looked Eva up and down, her eyes narrowing as she tried to place her. As recognition dawned, an unpleasant sneer crept onto her face. 'Oh, you're the decorator, aren't you?'

Ben didn't like her condescending tone and opened his mouth to speak but Eva squeezed his hand, shooting Kat a charming smile.

'That's right. Do let me know if you have any painting or decorating you need done – my rates are very reasonable and I'm sure Ben would be happy to recommend me.'

Kat stared at her for a moment then gave her a dismissive look, turning her attention to Ben. 'I haven't had a dance yet, Ben. Next one's mine when the band starts up?'

Ben felt his irritation rise again and he suddenly wanted to get out of the hall, wanted Eva to himself. 'Actually, we were just thinking about leaving.' He lifted an eyebrow at Eva for confirmation and was relieved to see her nod in agreement.

After a few handshakes and farewells Ben guided Eva out, weaving their way through the throng of bodies and out of the hall. The world fell silent and the evening air was cool after the heat of the hall as they walked back the way they had come earlier.

'You didn't mind leaving, did you?' he checked again with Eva.

'Not at all. I don't think my feet could have taken any more anyway. But didn't you want to hear the speeches?'

'I can live without them and I don't think the Professor will mind.'

'I liked him.' She smiled. 'So did you enjoy your first proper ceilidh then?'

'How could I not? The dancing was fun and the music was great – plus I got to dance with the most beautiful woman there.' He caught her hand and brought it to his lips. 'Thank you for coming with me.'

Eva glanced sideways at him from under her lashes, looking adorably shy before replying. 'Thanks for asking for me – it was great fun.'

Since the night of the storm Ben felt as if something had been unleashed in him. Not just his physical attraction to Eva but an emotional connection to her also. He had held himself back, worried that Eva had been on her own since losing her husband because she still loved him. He had been wary about treading on his memory but knowing Paul hadn't been the love of her life filled him with hope and excitement.

He could see that she had worked hard to get the life she had. He didn't want to jeopardize her and Jamie's stable world and he'd wrestled with his feelings but tonight, it felt like a physical impossibility to ignore those feelings.

Ben kept hold of her hand and their bodies drew closer. The night was clear and Ben automatically looked up. There was a large pale moon and the sky was pinpricked with thousands of twinkling stars. 'Do you know that Scotland is one of the best places in the world to stargaze?' he asked.

'Is it something to do with long winter nights?'

'That's one of the reasons.' He smiled. 'It's also because Scotland has a low population density so there's less light pollution, which makes it easier to see.'

Ben stopped walking and slipped his hand around Eva's waist, pointing with his free hand to a particular point in the sky. 'Can you see the Big Dipper?'

Eva looked up, her eyes roaming the darkness before nodding after a few moments.

'Now, focus in on the point where the handle of the big dipper meets the cup and draw an imaginary line from that point to the last star in the handle of the Little Dipper across from it.'

'Ok-kay, think I got it.'

'That line goes right through Cassiopeia – do you see? Those five bright stars making a W shape?' He traced the shape with his finger, watching Eva as her eyes scanned the sky until suddenly her face burst into a delighted smile as she recognized the formation.

'I see it!'

'That's Cassiopeia, a constellation in the northern sky.'

'Wow. Why's it called Cassiopeia?'

'Traditionally constellations are named after a mythological figure. Cassiopeia was supposed to be a vain queen who boasted about her unrivalled beauty.'

'Really?'

Ben gazed at Eva, who didn't seem to have a shred of vanity or to be aware of just how beautiful she was and it was driving him crazy. She was looking at him now, her green gaze intense and her lips slightly parted. He gently pulled her in towards him and tipped her chin with his finger, moving it towards his face so that their mouths were tantalizingly close.

'I don't think you have any idea how beautiful you are.' He brushed his mouth against hers.

'I don't?' she mumbled, her body moving in closer.

Ben felt consumed by a need for the feel of her and knew it was impossible for him to ignore the rush of desire invading every inch of his body. His finger trailed along her collarbone, up her neck and then around the shape of her lips. Very slowly he cupped her face and looked deep into her eyes, needing to know if she felt the same. She stared back into his eyes and answered his unspoken question by bringing her lips up to meet his again, her hands sliding to the back of his neck.

This time the kiss was long and deep. He heard her murmur his name and as she moved herself closer into him he felt the softness of her body against him and the feeling was so much more than he ever could have imagined.

Chapter Eleven

Eva's world felt different. She was waking in the same bed, in the same house but instead of turning to check the time, she turned the other way to see Ben lying beside her. In the soft morning light still half asleep, Eva could almost believe it was all a dream. But the gentle fall and rise of his chest told her it was real. She could reach out and touch him if she wanted. But for now, she allowed herself a few moments to luxuriate in simply studying his sleeping form, content to watch him as memories from the previous evening flitted pleasurably through her mind.

Last night, just for those few hours she had felt different. She had felt carefree in a way she hadn't for years. She hadn't been a mother, a widow, a business owner. Just herself, Eva. She had been transported to another world, a world of dancing and laughing and Ben. They had stumbled upstairs touching and teasing – Eva making Ben guess which door led to her bedroom. Then they had fallen silent, nervous to take the next step. She had felt madly self-conscious about her body, unsure she would know what to do.

But when Ben had gently removed Eva's dress, the look on his face told her she needn't have worried.

His eyes devoured her body and Eva had fallen into his arms, their lovemaking urgent and frantic as they discovered and explored each other. And then later Ben had made love to her again, this time slowly – the most sensual experience Eva had ever known – until finally they had fallen asleep.

Now she stretched out and sighed softly. No Jamie, no guests. Just her and Ben and it felt wonderful. Deep down she knew this was something she hadn't come close to before. She thought of Paul, how he had swept her away in a tide of excitement. She felt guilty for thinking it – he was the father of her child after all – but he hadn't aroused the feelings now engulfing Eva. It scared her, excited her. It made her feel strong yet vulnerable. It made her want to reach out and grab it and yet at the same time run and hide from it.

She knew she could get hurt so badly. She felt like something in her was awakening for the first time and she loved and hated Ben at the same time for making her feel like this. She could see now all the barriers she had built to keep herself safe and knew in one night Ben had smashed them all down.

She studied him for a few moments, her eyes savouring his toned, lean body, which had brought her such joy last night. And then she felt the cold hand of reality begin to slide over her. Anxiety and doubt crept in as she wondered what would happen now. What had she done? Quietly she slipped out of bed, pulled a T-shirt over her head, padded through to the bathroom, and looked at herself in the mirror. Her eyes held an undeniable sparkle and her skin glowed. It was still quite early but she knew Heather would be up – she was a fellow lark; the woman never slept in.

'Hi, Eva. Everything all right?' Eva smiled at the sound of her friend's voice.

'I'm a bad mother.'

'Okay. And why's that exactly?'

'Ben's in my bed!'

Her friend only missed a single beat before responding. 'And how does that make you a bad mother exactly?'

'My son goes away for the first time ever and I bring a man home! What kind of a mother does that make me?'

'Er, the human red-blooded kind?'

'Well you would say that. But I feel like a terrible human at the moment.'

'Eva, think about this. Ben's a nice person isn't he? He's intelligent ... oh yes and he's flipping gorgeous. You're probably just in shock this has happened. Please, Eva, just for once, enjoy the moment.'

Eva felt her shoulders relax, allowing Heather's words to infiltrate some part of her brain. 'You're right.'

'You shouldn't be talking to me. Go and be with him. I'm assuming underneath all that worry, you have a huge smile on your face?'

Despite herself, Eva grinned. 'Maybe,' she conceded.

After she hung up Eva went to find Hamish who had miraculously stayed in his basket all night. He was probably in shock too if he had witnessed anything. She gave him his breakfast and let him out in the garden for a few minutes, as she took a few breaths of fresh air.

She was slightly hungover and not just from alcohol. She took a long drink of cold water, giving herself a moment of reflection. She'd have to think carefully about what to tell Jamie. But tell him what? What happened had been amazing but it didn't necessarily mean anything, did it? No promises had been made. The connection between them was undeniable but it had all happened so quickly. Had she given in to her physical desires too soon? Remembering Heather's words she decided now wasn't the time to analyse it. There would plenty of time for that later.

Tiptoeing back into the bedroom she slid beneath the covers and stared over at Ben, amazed how beautiful he looked with his rumpled dark hair and eyelashes casting shadows on his cheeks. His body shifted and his eyes – those dark gorgeous eyes – slowly opened and gazed at her. For a long moment their eyes locked and then a slow sexy smile spread across his lips. What was he thinking? She felt suddenly shy, despite what they had shared last night. Without speaking he pulled her in to him, kissing her.

'Morning to you too,' she replied when they eventually parted. 'Are you hungry?'

'Yeah, starving actually,' he replied with a lopsided grin.

'Must have been all that dancing,'

'Must have been.' He smiled wickedly.

As they moved from the bed, Eva recited her breakfast menu in an exaggerated formal voice. 'There's a choice of traditional full Scottish breakfast or you may prefer our continental choice of warm rolls, jams, and seasonal fruits ...' Eva stopped, lifting an eyebrow. 'But for special guests I can arrange something extra …' She giggled as Ben groaned.

'I tell you what, how about omelettes?' Ben suggested, pulling on his shirt. 'They're about the only thing I can make – kind of my signature dish.'

'Sounds good.'

In the kitchen, Ben set about whisking eggs while Eva filled the teapot with boiling water and made toast. She turned to find Ben staring at her. 'What?'

'I hope that's not how you usually look when you make breakfast for your guests.'

Eva looked down at her crumpled T-shirt. 'Um, definitely not.'

'That's all right then.' He came behind her and nuzzled her neck. She turned to face him and as he peppered her throat with kisses, Eva was tempted to forget all about breakfast. Only the imminent threat of burning toast broke them apart.

Their breakfast of eggs, hot buttered toast, and mugs of tea was delicious and they both ate hungrily. She glanced over at Ben and felt an overwhelming sense of happiness. She decided now wasn't the time to overthink things. Whatever this did or didn't mean, she simply wanted to enjoy this moment.

That moment was abruptly shattered by the sound of the doorbell ringing. She glanced at the clock. Who would be calling so early on a Saturday morning? Her first thought was Jamie and the cold dread she felt must have shown on her face. Ben squeezed her hand for a second.

'Don't look so worried. You answer the door and I'll stay here.' Eva hurriedly ran a hand through her hair, took a deep breath, and opened the door to find herself face to face with her sister.

'Sarah?'

Eva didn't know what shocked her more – the fact her sister was standing at her door on Saturday morning or that she looked utterly distraught, tears running down her face. Sarah didn't usually do emotion. And she certainly didn't do crying.

'Sarah, what's happened?'

'It's Mum …' Sarah gulped. 'She's … I saw them –' Her voice broke into a sob.

'Mum? Is she all right?' Eva felt the colour drain from her face. Her sister took an enormous sniff and shook her head.

'Mum's got a boyfriend!'

Her words hung in the air for a second and then her shoulders slumped. So many things about that sentence didn't sound right, Eva wasn't sure how to respond. A hundred thoughts whirled through her mind, most of them incredulous. She also had a sudden terrible urge to burst out laughing. Eva stood in shocked silence for a moment before realizing Sarah was still standing on the doorstep and Hamish had just arrived to investigate what all the fuss was about.

'Come in, come in. Don't say anything else just now.' With Ben in the kitchen, Eva ushered her sister into the living room. She opened the blinds and lit the fire, trying to make the room feel as cosy as possible. Sarah perched on the edge of the sofa, emitting little sobs every now and again.

Eva was acutely aware of her own appearance and hoped she didn't look as dishevelled as she felt. Her body ached at all the unfamiliar activity, her lips felt stung, and despite her sister's obvious distress, she felt gloriously alive, as if her body was hugging a lovely secret to itself. But she couldn't deal with her sister looking like this and with Ben in the house.

'Just give me a minute and I'll er, go and change. Then you can tell me what's happened.'

'Where's Jamie?' Sarah asked vaguely, looking around as if he would suddenly pop up from behind the furniture.

'He's at the activity weekend.' Now wasn't the time to point out that she had mentioned that to her only a matter of days ago. Eva headed back into the kitchen, trying to picture her mother with a boyfriend but just couldn't do it.

Ben was buttoning up his shirt when Eva returned to the kitchen. Her eyes were drawn to the muscular contours of his chest, which were now so achingly familiar, and sent a small shiver up her spine. God, he looked gorgeous. Forcing herself to concentrate, she explained who her unexpected guest was.

'My sister is here,' Eva whispered. 'Apparently my mother has a boyfriend.' Ben shot her such a quizzical look Eva couldn't help giggling. 'Knowing my sister, it could be nothing. She's probably got hold of the wrong end of the stick or something. She's pretty upset … it's a bit awkward and er –'

'And you don't want her to see me?'

'Maybe not the best time for introductions. I'm sorry, I really didn't expect this to happen.'

'You do what you have to, don't worry about me. I'll sneak out the back door – not something I've had to do before,' he said, winking at her.

'Oh God, I'm sorry about this,' Eva said trying to cover her disappointment. This wasn't exactly how she hoped today might unfold. Ben hooked his finger under her chin and tilted it upwards. He bent his head down and kissed her thoroughly, leaving her feeling slightly dazed and wishing things hadn't been brought to such an abrupt end. It felt farcical to be smuggling a man out of the house – she was a grown woman in her own home.

After Ben left, Eva quickly dressed and returned to Sarah, who appeared not to have moved an inch. She sat down beside her, speaking quietly. 'So do you want to talk? Tell me what happened?'

Sarah let out a dramatic sigh, her mouth quivering for a moment as she found her voice. 'You know Mum got a new kitchen fitted recently?'

'Yes, she seemed very happy with it.' Eva frowned, wondering where this was going.

'Last night I called round to Mum's. I don't usually go to hers on a Friday night but I'd lost a big case at work.' She paused, twisting a ring round and round her finger.

'Anyway, I thought I'd go and see Mum, take a bottle of wine, thinking we could just chat. I phoned her first but there was no answer so I thought she must be with her friend Deidre. They sometimes meet on a Friday afternoon and go shopping. I decided to let myself in and wait for her. But when I went in the house –' Sarah gulped, her eyes blinking back tears as she came to the painful part. 'I saw Mum and, and – him in the living room. They were on the sofa and they were, well they –' She stopped, unable to continue.

Eva's mouth hung open. 'What, Mum and the kitchen fitter?' she said incredulously.

'Not the fitter.' Sarah glowered, shaking her head in frustration at Eva's inability to keep up. 'The man who owns the kitchen company.'

'Oh, I see.' Well, that sounded slightly more plausible.

'I had seen him at her house – every time I went he seemed to be there, showing Mum different designs and layouts for the kitchen.'

Eva remembered how well Helen had looked last time she'd seen her, a definite glow about her. Now she knew why. 'So what happened next?'

'Mum was flustered, you know. Her hair was all over the place, a total mess.' She shook her head sadly.

'And, um, what were they doing exactly? You know, were they actually –?'

Sarah looked at Eva in horror. 'No! They broke apart when I came in. Mum asked me to stay for a drink – tried to act all normal.'

'And then what happened?'

'We sat and had a drink together. Made polite conversation – it was awful. Then I left and went home. I tried to sleep but couldn't. So this morning I got in the car and came here.'

Eva pondered exactly why Sarah had come here. Had she come all this way, after all this time, just to tell her that their mum had a boyfriend? Evidently she was upset about it but Eva couldn't help sensing there was something more to it. She felt a surge of pity for Sarah. She looked totally worn out and Eva realized it was going to be difficult to make any sense of anything while Sarah was clearly so exhausted.

'Listen, would you like to have a lie-down? You haven't slept and things always seem worse when you're tired.' Eva thought she might resist but Sarah immediately acquiesced. She led the way upstairs showing Sarah into her coastal-themed bedroom, which was ready for the guest arriving on Monday.

Opening the door Eva allowed herself a quiet moment of satisfaction seeing the look on Sarah's face as she registered the room. The bed was made up with plump pillows and crisp fresh navy and cream bedding. Eva drew the curtains as Sarah lay down on the bed. Eva covered her with a spare blanket and she was asleep in seconds.

***

Ben started to run as soon his feet hit the sand. He'd changed into his running gear after leaving Eva's and headed straight to the beach, glad it was practically empty and no one could see him because he was sure he was grinning like an idiot. But he was one very happy, satisfied idiot. He couldn't remember ever feeling like this before. He hadn't truly appreciated just how unhappy he had become until now, as if something had been broken and now it was fixed.

He knew there were implications from what happened last night, the most important being Jamie. But he would let Eva decide how to handle things on that front. Last night with Eva had been incredible and the intensity of their passion had surprised him. His only regret was the sudden ending this morning. Still, there would time in the future … at least he certainly hoped there would be.

He'd always kept himself reasonably fit but recently he hadn't done much exercise. Today he felt physically strong and energized, as if he could run for ever. He picked up his pace and lengthened his stride, wanting to push himself and feel the strength of his own body. He ran until his lungs and muscles screamed in protest and eventually he allowed his body to slow down.

He stopped and bent over, resting his hands on his knees, letting his breathing return to normal. He straightened up and stretched and began to walk back to his house. In the kitchen he filled a glass with water and drank thirstily, wondering how Eva was getting on with her sister. Halfway up the stairs his phone rang and his heart plummeted when he saw the caller ID. 'Hello, Arthur?'

'Hello, Ben. I'm sorry to bother you, especially at the weekend.' Ben heard the older man's voice, knowing it would be impossible for him to bother Ben in any way.

Arthur and his wife Mary lived next door to the house where Ben had grown up and had been family friends for years. Arthur was a true gentleman, from a different generation. The house was a bungalow in a quiet cul-de-sac in St Albans near London. Ben hadn't known what to do with it after his mother had moved into the care home – even kidding himself that one day she might return. After a while he'd handed over the property to a letting company who had secured a long-term let. The arrangement had worked well but the tenants had recently moved out.

Having it lying empty wasn't ideal but Ben couldn't bring himself to sell it and had been putting off making any decisions. Arthur had always kept a spare set of keys and an unofficial eye on the place and Ben knew he'd only be phoning if there was a problem. He braced himself for bad news.

'There's been a break-in, Ben. I called the police and luckily it looks like they were disturbed. They don't seem to have taken anything – not that I could see anyway.'

Ben rubbed a hand over his face. 'Do you know how they broke in?' he asked.

'Back of the house – they broke a panel of glass in a downstairs window. I've managed to board it up for now – but obviously it needs to be fixed properly.'

'Of course.' The thought of Arthur dealing with it horrified Ben. He felt something pull in him and a sense of urgency take hold. 'Thanks for taking care of it, Arthur – I'm so sorry you've had to deal with this.'

After the call finished, Ben did some quick thinking. It was still early. If he drove to the airport and managed to get a flight to London, he could be in St Albans by this evening. The conference was this coming week and students had been given a study week so at least he didn't have any teaching. He'd send an email to the Professor and the department secretary explaining the situation. He should only be away for a couple of days.

Although the break-in was bad news, in some ways Ben felt relieved, knowing it had galvanized him into action. Finally, he was going to face his old home.

Chapter Twelve

Eva was furiously chopping vegetables. She had no idea what she was making, but it was comforting having something simmering on the stove and keeping her hands busy was helping her cope with what was feeling like a very surreal day.

After she had left Sarah sleeping earlier she had taken a quick shower and dressed. She'd let Hamish out for a sniff around the garden while she fed the chickens and then she returned to the kitchen to hide the evidence of breakfast for two. She had grabbed plates and cups, throwing them in the dishwasher and wiping away crumbs. All perfectly normal breakfast things but to Eva they somehow screamed of the intimacy she had shared with Ben.

Part of her resented having to rush around tidying up just because Sarah had decided to show up after all this time. But what choice did she have? She certainly didn't want Sarah knowing Ben had stayed the night – not yet anyway. She swiped onions and carrots from the chopping board into the pan, deciding to make soup. She was just adding celery when Sarah appeared at the kitchen door.

Although she was still pale and puffy-eyed she appeared much more composed. Her features had settled back into their usual impassive expression and her lips were pursed together into such a tight line Eva wondered if she was now regretting her earlier outburst, perhaps regretting coming here at all.

'I took a shower,' she informed Eva. 'I used those little bottle things you had.' The little bottles in question being the locally sourced organic toiletries it had taken Eva an age to source and were actually quite expensive. Eva had no problem with her using the guest toiletries but wouldn't mind her sounding a little more gracious about it.

'That's fine,' she replied evenly, gripping the wooden spoon in her hand tightly.

Sarah's eyes scanned the room as she came in, pausing to look intently at the various photographs dotted about. Images of Jamie wearing his school uniform on his first day at school, another of Jamie and Fraser playing on the beach. Eva wondered what she was thinking.

Seeing her sister in her kitchen Eva was struck by how different they appeared. Sarah's clothes – impeccably cut dark blue trousers and a beautifully soft-looking cream jumper – appeared wrinkle free despite her lie-down and they reeked of unmistakable quality. Eva looked down at her own jeans and rubbed at a dark mysterious stain that could well be animal-related.

'Feeling better now?' Eva asked.

'I'm fine,' Sarah replied flatly.

'I'll make us some coffee,' Eva said. As she busied herself finding cups Eva wondered where on earth to start, sure that anything she said would come out sounding wrong. Sarah was clearly feeling the injured party here and Eva couldn't help feel sorry for her. But she also knew that if they were going to come anywhere close to having a reasonable conversation – something they had been incapable of recently – Sarah would have to play her part.

She turned the heat down under the pot on the stove and joined Sarah at the table with coffee. 'Does Mum know you're here?' she asked.

Sarah shrugged. 'I left a message on her answering machine to let her know I'd be here for the night.'

'Oh, so you're staying the night?' Eva swallowed down her irritation at her sister's presumption.

'Is that a problem?' Sarah eyed her coolly.

'No, no. I have guests arriving on Monday though so I might have a few things to do.' Sarah didn't appear overly interested and Eva's eyes darted to the clock above the door to check it was afternoon and therefore acceptable to have a drink. If Sarah was staying the night, then alcohol was called for.

'Actually, how about a glass of wine?' she suggested. Sarah nodded and Eva swapped the coffee cups for glasses and a bottle of white.

'So, Mum and this man –' Eva began.

'George Cartwright.'

'George Cartwright,' Eva repeated. 'Do you think it's serious?'

'I don't know. Maybe. They certainly look happy together.' She let out a little huff.

'I understand what a shock it must have been,' Eva responded gently. 'To see Mum with a man after all this time. But if she's happy, isn't that a good thing?'

Sarah blinked as if not understanding the question. 'How can it be a good thing?'

'Well, for Mum to have someone.'

'But she has me!' Sarah exclaimed petulantly.

Eva fiddled with her bracelet, not sure what to say. She was struggling to see the problem. If their mother was in a relationship, then wasn't it her business? She couldn't really see the problem but clearly there was one to Sarah. But as Eva glanced sideways at Sarah, she saw genuine anguish on her face. Whatever the rights and wrongs of the situation, Sarah had come to her in her moment of need. Could this be the chance for them to build a few bridges between them?

Putting aside any uncharitable thoughts – mostly that Sarah was acting like a spoilt brat stamping her feet because Mum dared to have a life – Eva tried to adopt a gentle approach.

'I know you've been there for Mum and have done so much for her and she appreciates that. But just because she has a relationship with a man doesn't mean you won't still be part of her life. It might not even be serious; it might not last. Maybe it's just a … a fling?' After all, why shouldn't women in their sixties have flings?

Sarah's shoulders suddenly slumped as if all the life had been taken from her.

'I don't know. I suppose so. But where does it leave me?' she asked, her voice full of self-pity. Eva was taken aback to hear her usually so confident sister sounding so vulnerable and quite frankly, a bit pathetic. Eva's instinct was to reach out and put an arm around her but was afraid it wouldn't be welcome.

'Well, you have your career ...' Eva stopped, not sure what else to say. The gulf created by years of non-communication was blindingly obvious.

'Oh yes, my wonderful career,' Sarah spat out sarcastically.

'But you love your work! You're always so busy and ... involved.'

Eva blinked in surprise as her sister rounded on her. 'You really don't get it do you?'

'No, I don't think I do. So why don't you tell me.'

'Let me ask you something.' Sarah looked at Eva, her eyes suddenly flaring with anger. 'Why did you go away after Dad died?'

Wow, she hadn't seen that coming. It sounded like a question she'd been waiting to ask for a long time. Eva looked down and blinked, giving herself time before meeting Sarah's direct gaze.

'After Dad died, you moved back from Aberdeen and bought the house near Mum's. You both seemed happy with that arrangement; you had each other.' She shook her head, recalling how terrible that time was. While Sarah went shopping with their mother, Eva had preferred to stay at home with their dad. With the radio on and a flask of tea, they'd potter about in the shed – the one place Helen Devine didn't rule or dominate – making things or planting seeds.

'You were always closer to Mum than me but I didn't have Dad any more. Mum seemed to have my life all mapped out – do you remember that horrible office where I was working?' Eva could vividly recall the day Paul asked her to join him in France. It had been a rainy Monday, a week after their father's funeral and Mr Sinclair had unceremoniously dumped a pile of filing on Eva's desk.

'When Paul said he could get me a job waitressing in France, I didn't really think about you too much if I'm honest. I thought you were happy. You had Mum and your career. I just went,' she finished with a shrug.

'Yeah, well while you went off, I built my life around Mum.'

'I thought that's what you wanted.'

Sarah lowered her head and examined her nails. 'I thought you might have come back after Paul died,' she said quietly.

'What, so Mum could tell me every day what a mess I'd made of my life? Anyway, I had Jamie to think of. Buying the guest house was my way of getting on with my life. I needed to find a way to support myself and as Mum was so keen to point out, I didn't have any qualifications.' Eva topped up their glasses and regarded Sarah.

'Do you know one of the reasons I was so determined to make the guest house work was because of you?'

'Me?' Now it was Sarah's turn to look shocked.

'Do you know how many times Mum compared me to you? How many times she made me feel inadequate because I didn't have a glittering career? Always holding you up as the perfect daughter. I wanted her to see that I could make something of my life as well.' There was a pause and Sarah stared down into her wine glass.

'I – I had no idea you felt like that,' she said eventually.

'Look, I don't mean to sound churlish. You have done well, Sarah. And it's right that Mum is proud of you. It's just ... sometimes it was difficult for me. It felt as though all Mum did was – I don't know, smother you with praise.'

Eva heard Sarah exhale deeply. 'You're right.'

'You're agreeing with me?'

'You don't need to sound quite so shocked.' Sarah leaned back in her seat, seeming to gather herself. 'Do you remember that little silver necklace Mum gave me?'

'The one with the heart on it? I loved that necklace. I was so jealous of you.'

'Do you know why Mum got it for me?'

Eva scrunched up her face, thinking. 'I don't remember.'

'I was in first year at high school and I brought home my first report card. I'd done well in all my subjects and Mum was so pleased with me. She bought me that necklace for doing so well. The better I did, the happier she seemed with me. After that, I always felt pressure to do well. Through university, my job ... everything I did, everything I do. I'm always scared if I don't make Mum happy then somehow I've failed.'

Eva had no idea Sarah had felt under so much pressure. She'd always assumed her sister had been happy with her career and their mother's adulation. If Sarah's face was anything to go by, then she was feeling as stunned as she was, thought Eva. After years of hardly speaking, there was a slightly uneasy silence as they both tried to compute the words now sitting between them.

When Hamish trotted over to Eva making it clear he needed out, Eva could have kissed him for providing a diversion. She stood up quickly, almost knocking her chair backwards. 'I better let Hamish out,' she muttered.

The sky had darkened and Sarah stared out of the window. Eva could just make out Hamish's tail wagging in the garden as he checked the chickens and then found something to sniff by the fence that divided her garden from Ben's. She wondered what Ben was doing and felt a glow of warmth spread through her just thinking of him.

Once Hamish came bounding back in Eva thought it might be wise for them to eat something. She found some quiche in the fridge and turned up the heat under the soup. Leaning against the worktop, she glanced over at Sarah.

'So the case you lost, was it an important one?'

Sarah gave a rueful laugh. 'They're all important. But I didn't expect to lose this one – I keep going over and over it in my mind. Was it my fault – was there something more I could have done?'

'I think you're being too hard on yourself. I'm sure it wasn't your fault.'

'It seems to get harder, you know? The constant deadlines, keeping up with the legislation ... always being available for clients. Sometimes it feels like such an effort.'

Eva ladled soup into bowls and brought them over to the table along with plates of oatcakes and cheese, thinking how odd it was to hear Sarah sounding so despondent.

'Sounds to me like you might need a proper break from everything.'

'That's what Jon said,' Sarah said quietly.

'Jon?'

Sarah swallowed hard as if she were on the verge of tears. 'You don't want to know,' she said bitterly.

'I do, Sarah. Please tell me.'

Sarah absently stirred her spoon in her bowl. 'Jon works for our firm's Holland office. He came on a secondment for six months. We got to know each other quite well ...' She paused. 'Anyway, he does quite a bit of pro-bono work –'

'Pro-bono?'

'Basically it's doing free legal work for people who wouldn't otherwise be able to afford it. While he was in Edinburgh he got involved in setting up a legal advice centre for residents in a homeless shelter – so they would be able to get legal assistance for things like welfare and family law. I helped him with some of the work.'

'Sounds like a decent thing to do.'

'Yeah, well he was a decent guy. Not like anyone I've ever met. He made me see things differently. See my life differently.' She sat back in her seat, her expression changing. 'Then his six months was up and he returned to Holland. Before he left, he asked me to go with him.'

Eva's eyes widened with surprise. 'And?'

'And nothing.' She shrugged. 'I told him I couldn't go.'

'Oh, Sarah, how long ago was this?'

'A few weeks ago.'

'Why did you say no?' Eva asked gently.

'I wouldn't leave Mum on her own. I said no without even thinking about it.'

Eva now understood why seeing Helen with someone must have been so difficult for her, after giving up the chance of her own relationship.

'Would you like to see him again?'

'I don't know. I guess so. But I haven't spoken to him since he left.'

'Was he nice?' Eva gave her a little smile.

'Yeah, he was lovely.'

'If Mum does have someone – a partner, boyfriend, or whatever – doesn't that make it easier for you now? You could go to Holland if you wanted. I'd be here for Mum – you know that. I'm not right beside her but I don't mind making the drive to see her; it's not that long. Or she could come here, although I've given up asking.'

Sarah didn't answer immediately and then she shrugged helplessly. 'I don't know what to think or what I'm going to do now,' she said with a sigh.

Eva's own thoughts tumbled about in her head as she struggled to process the last twenty-four hours. It looked like it was going to be a long night.

***

The next morning Eva and Sarah strolled through the winter market, browsing stalls selling hand-made toys, jewellery, and candles. They warmed up with cups of hot chocolate and then made their way to the beach, Sarah having swapped her designer heels for a pair of Eva's wellies before they left the house.

The water was cold and choppy-looking and the sky overcast. Eva let Hamish off his lead and they watched him gallop to the water's edge. Eva inhaled deeply, glad to be in the fresh air. Yesterday had been a long, strange day. Last night she and Sarah had talked some more although at times it felt as if they were treading carefully around each other, neither wanting to say the wrong thing.

Discovering a forgotten bottle of wine in the kitchen and a Sandra Bullock film on TV had gone a long way to helping them pass the evening before tiredness had finally kicked in and they had headed to bed.

But Eva had tossed and turned, going over the day's events in her mind. She could hardly believe she had started the day waking next to Ben and when she finally fell asleep, it was with her head resting on the pillow where he had slept. When she'd woken this morning there was a text from him saying he'd had to fly to London unexpectedly.

Eva had bit down a surge of disappointment. She didn't know what she had hoped for after their night together but a short text message from the other end of the country felt a long way off it. She started a reply, trying to sound casual and flirty but worried it came over as needy and then gave up, not really knowing what she wanted to say or how to say it.

She had woken Sarah this morning, grateful they seemed to have turned a corner in their relationship. Eva had seen glimpses of her old sister and realized they had both made mistakes. They had stopped communicating but now they were talking again, which was the most important thing. Eva knew it would take more than this weekend. They couldn't wipe away all the hurt in one clean sweep but they had made a good start.

'The bedroom was really comfortable,' Sarah commented now as they continued along the beach.

'Thanks,' Eva replied.

'You know, Mum is proud of you.'

Eva gave a small huff. 'You think?'

'I've heard her telling her friends about your business.'

'Really? I wonder why she can't just say it to my face then.'

'You know what she's like: she's always been a bit of a snob.'

'Suppose.' Eva sniggered, throwing a stick for Hamish, and they watched him sprint after it.

'You always did want a dog,' Sarah recalled. 'You asked Mum over and over but there was no way she was ever going to get one.'

Eva smiled at the memory. 'I gave up asking eventually. Now I'm beginning to think Mum had the right idea.'

'What made you get a dog now then?'

'Jamie,' Eva replied simply. 'During summer we can't go on holiday because of the business and most of his friends have brothers or sisters, so I suppose I thought it would be good for him – a companion of sorts.'

Sarah regarded her, a frown appearing on her smooth forehead. 'You've don't have holidays?'

'We've had the odd night away but apart from that, no.'

Sarah's head was down as they continued to walk, appearing deep in thought. 'I've been a crap aunt, haven't I?' she suddenly announced.

The odd expensive present aside, Eva thought it was a pretty fair assessment but not wanting to rock their fragile truce she tried to sound supportive.

'Your career is very demanding – I understand that you don't have lots of free time.'

Sarah gave her head a little shake, frowning. 'Where did you say he was?'

'An activity weekend with his football team.' Eva felt a rush of joy thinking he'd be home soon. 'Are you sure you don't want to come and collect him with me? I'm sure he would love to see you.'

'No, I'd better get back but I'll see him another time soon.'

'So, what will you do now – about Jon and everything?'

'I don't know.' Sarah shrugged. 'Talk to Mum first I guess.'

Eva was tempted to share her own situation with Ben – whatever that might be – but Sarah clearly had enough to deal with for now. They continued along the beach for a few more minutes before deciding to turn back.

Eva called to Hamish, now in full flight racing along the water's edge with another dog, and waved to the dog owner whom she recognized. She turned to Sarah who was walking with her head down and Eva was filled with a sudden urgency for her sister to seize her opportunity of happiness.

'I really hope you can make this work, Sarah. If there's a chance for you to be happy, to have a life with someone, then I hope you take it. It's too precious to throw away.' Eva swallowed, surprised by the strength of emotion in her voice. 'Whatever you decide, I'm here for you,' she finished with a small smile. Her sister's expression gave nothing away and Eva could only hope her words might help in some way.

When Hamish finally returned they headed home. Eva glanced over at Ben's empty driveway, shrugging off the irrational niggle she felt. Instead, she thought of Jamie coming home.

Chapter Thirteen

Jamie appeared at the kitchen door with a look of hunger that Eva could spot at ten paces. 'Dinner's almost ready,' she told him before he started to raid the fridge. The cheese sauce was finished and now she was mixing it into the pasta. Apparently the food at the centre had been all right but what Jamie really wanted was his mum's home-made macaroni. Scattering some breadcrumbs and grated cheese on top Eva put the dish under the grill for a few minutes.

Jamie ambled over to the table with Hamish close by his side. After their enthusiastic reunion last night the two of them had been inseparable apart from when Jamie had to go to school this morning. 'You know, I'm sure you've grown,' Eva said tilting her head to the side.

'I was only away for two days, Mum, not two years.'

'Well, it felt like two years to me.' She smiled going over to him.

'Mum,' Jamie groaned, managing to dodge Eva's arms as she came over for yet another hug. She couldn't help it – she was so happy to have him home she felt like squeezing him every time she saw him.

Stepping off the bus last night, Jamie had looked somewhat bedraggled but Eva had been ecstatic to see him. Despite all her fretting, she could see how much he'd enjoyed himself. He'd been hyper on the drive home, describing in detail the thrills of his weekend. 'Honest – it was amazing, Mum. We did waterfall jumps and boulder hopping. But the abseiling was best.'

Eva had winced as he recounted being harnessed up and tipped backwards over the drop to descend the cliff face. Seeing his mother's face Jamie had reassured her. 'It was fine, Mum, there was a safety rope and the instructor watched me the whole time.'

When they'd arrived home, Jamie had taken a much-needed hot bath. Eva had tipped out his rucksack, creating a mound of muddy clothes, and put on the first of many washings. She'd been battling all day trying to get everything dry, draping clothes over radiators and exhausting the tumble dryer. Even though it was winter she'd hoped to hang out some washing but there was no chance of that. She had never known it to be so wet in St Andrews.

With the macaroni now bubbling and golden, Eva served a huge plateful to Jamie and joined him at the table, grateful for the seat. She'd been on her feet all day and exhaustion flooded her body. The day hadn't got off to a good start when she'd slept through the alarm – something she'd never done before – and woken with a throbbing head and gritty eyes. She wasn't sure if she was coming down with something or if it was just the weekend catching up with her.

She'd charged through to wake up Jamie, racing to get him ready for school in time, and felt as if she'd been trying to catch up with herself all day.

She had completed a final check of the bedrooms making sure they were fully ready. The beds were all made up, carpets hoovered, furniture dusted, and the en suites given a final clean. The first guest had arrived earlier before Jamie had come home from school and was already happily ensconced in her room.

Eva had exchanged emails with both guests, one male and one female, so she was able to deduce when she opened the door to a lady it was Miss Havers who had travelled from York. She carried a pile of books under one arm and a canvas bag in the other. In her sixties Eva guessed, with grey hair tucked behind her ears and rimless round glasses. She had a distracted air as if she was trying to remember something.

Eva had ushered her in out of the rain and showed her to her room, deciding to give her the front room that Sarah had recently vacated. Eva made sure she had everything she needed and Miss Havers had made it clear she was quite happy to be left alone.

'You all right, Mum?' Jamie broke into her reverie. 'You don't look so good.'

Eva knew she must look pretty awful to warrant a comment from her son. 'I'm fine, just tired, that's all. How's your macaroni?'

'Awesome.' He smiled with a nod of his head. Eva tilted her head, hearing sounds at the front door.

'That'll be our next guest,' she said to Jamie. 'Can you stay here with Hamish? I'll go and see to them.'

Eva pasted her best smile in place and swung opened the door. 'Good evening,' she said cheerfully. 'Welcome to West Sands guest house. You must be Mr Hargreaves?'

'Doctor Hargreaves actually,' Eva heard him mutter as he marched through the door carrying with him a briefcase, a wet umbrella, and a sense of entitlement. Over the years, Eva had learned to recognize problem guests. Thankfully, they were few and far between. Most of her guests were lovely, simply looking to relax, enjoy one or two nights away from home. But every now and then there was someone intent on never being happy. You could almost sense it – a look of derision that said nothing you do will be good enough.

At first Eva had agonized over these people, thinking it was something she was doing wrong. But time had taught her there was no pleasing some people and so it was with a sense of gloom that she now identified this guest as one of those people.

'I'm terribly sorry, *Doctor* Hargreaves. How was your journey?'

'A nightmare. I really don't know what's wrong with this country – why is it you can't travel from one place to the other without encountering some form of roadworks?'

Eva tutted sympathetically. 'Oh dear, I'm sorry you've not had a good journey.'

'And the blasted rain hasn't stopped for hours.' He shook his wet coat, clearly irritated by the weather too. Eva hung up his coat and asked him to sign a confirmation sheet with his details and located the keys for his room before leading the way upstairs. His beady little eyes darted about like a bird's as if he was looking for something.

'Do you do food?'

'We only serve breakfast but I can recommend a good choice of restaurants, which are all very near. I can let you see some of their menus if you wish.'

'I can assure you I am not going back out in that rain.'

Eva knew her job was to soothe the harassed traveller but she was pretty certain even if his journey and the weather had been perfect, Doctor Hargreaves would still find something to complain about.

'Your room does have tea and coffee making facilities,' she said politely pointing to the kettle and china cups on the table. Eva had also left a welcome tray with some fresh fruit and shortbread biscuits. 'Your room has colour TV and there's a CD/radio alarm. I'm usually about but my mobile number is on the information sheet if you need anything –'

Eva wasn't sure how it happened but Hamish appeared out of nowhere, charged into the room, and took a flying leap on to the bed. Dr Hargreaves's face turned puce and Eva thought for one terrible moment he was going to have a seizure of some sort.

'Hamish! Off now! I'm so sorry.' Eva hauled Hamish off the bed.

'You – you have a dog in here?' he said in horror. A sudden terrible thought dawned on Eva.

'You're not allergic, are you?'

'What? No,' he replied gruffly. 'But I can't stand dogs, especially in a bedroom.'

200

'Of course, I'm so sorry. He's a family pet and this should never have happened. He won't bother you again I can assure you.' Oh dear, this was not going well. 'Come on, boy, out of here.' Eva gently shoved him out into the hall, trying to think of a way to compensate Dr Hargreaves for his upset. Inspiration came to Eva in the form of food.

'I'm so sorry again. Seeing as it's just a terrible night and you don't want to go back out, please let me bring some food to your room, as a way of apology. I have home-made soup and bread and some local cheese if that's acceptable?'

'Very well,' he harrumphed turning his back on her.

Eva found Jamie looking sheepish in his bedroom with an equally guilty-looking Hamish sitting beside him. 'How did that happen?' she snapped. 'Actually, you know what, don't tell me.' Now wasn't the time for a cross-examination about how Hamish ended up in a guest's room – that was a conversation for another time. 'Hamish hasn't been out for a walk today. Can you take him out now please while I make some food and get the guest settled?'

'Yeah, all right. Come on, boy,' Jamie agreed, knowing Eva's tone wasn't one to be argued with.

In the kitchen, Eva took a deep breath and set about heating some home-made soup and defrosting bread she had in the freezer. She had discovered the joys of making bread shortly after she'd moved to St Andrews. There was nothing like the aroma of freshly baked bread drifting through the house and her guests seem to love it. She heard Jamie leave by the front door as she started to assemble a tray with the improvised meal for Dr Hargreaves.

With the bread defrosted, Eva began to cut slices of cheese, wondering if she had a temperature. The pain in her head had intensified and she was feeling distinctly hot and bothered. A gust of wind rattling against the window made her jump. She lost concentration for a split second and the knife slipped in her hand, slashing across her finger. Damn! She didn't need to look to know it was a deep cut.

She closed her eyes as a wave of nausea hit her. She quickly grabbed a tissue, wrapped it round the wound, and fetched the first-aid box. She dressed the wound, washed her hands, and hurried upstairs with the tray before Dr Hargreaves wondered where she had got to.

***

The captain of Ben's flight back to Edinburgh had just warned passengers to expect a bumpy landing due to high winds. Ben didn't care if the plane flew backwards just as long they landed and the sooner the better. An urgency to see Eva consumed him. He needed to speak to her, to hold her. He wanted to hear all about Jamie's trip. He smiled thinking how happy she would be to have him home.

As the plane began its descent through the thick blanket of grey cloud, Ben reflected on the last two days. It had been busy and painful at times, but now his sense of relief was palpable.

The hardest part had been taking that first step into the house again. The memory of the day he had led his mother out of the house to take her to the care home was as crushingly painful as ever. All the years she had lovingly looked after Ben, now in a cruel reversal of roles it was her trusting him. He didn't know exactly what her brain was able to compute – it seemed to change every day – but he hoped with all his heart she didn't realize he was taking her to a place full of strangers to care for her.

The house had looked more or less the same when he walked in. Everything was neat and tidy, but tired and worn-looking. Before the tenants had moved in Ben had decluttered the house, leaving only the large pieces of furniture. He'd taken a few bits and pieces and personal items but everything else was stored in the attic.

He'd walked from room to room and at first the rush of memories had overwhelmed him. But instead of blocking them as he'd done so often in the past, he let them in, remembering all the happy moments of their family life. His dad coming home early from work so they could kick a ball about in the back garden, chatting about their days over mealtimes. Ben's friends coming over to play – his mother had always been happy to fill the house with his friends, even more so after his dad had died.

He smiled, thinking how his mother would have loved Eva. Loved that she was practical, independent, loving, and caring – those were things that would matter to her.

On a practical level, there had been plenty to do. Arthur had been more than willing to help, driving them to a DIY store where they bought extra security lighting. He'd managed to get an emergency locksmith to upgrade all the locks and a glazier to fix the broken glass.

He'd taken Arthur and Mary out to dinner to a local restaurant – it was the least he could do – and this morning when Arthur had asked him what his plans were, Ben had replied truthfully he didn't know yet but would very soon. He wanted all his future decisions to involve Eva and he couldn't wait to get back to her.

From that very first moment he'd met Eva something had pulled him in. Every time they met, he'd wanted more. At first he'd struggled with the knowledge a woman he'd just met could make him feel the way he did. It hadn't exactly been the best of timings. The end of his relationship, moving, and starting a new job, the last thing he had expected was to find true love. His life with Samantha felt a million years away and he was amazed at how little he thought of her now.

With hindsight he could see what was blatantly obvious: that their relationship was never going to last. He had never given his heart to Samantha, never truly loved her, and he doubted she ever really loved him. In some ways maybe they had both been guilty of deceiving each other, clinging to each other as a means to an end. He hoped Samantha found happiness and if she was really lucky, found someone she loved too. Because Ben now knew he loved Eva with everything he had.

For the past five years Ben's life had been at a standstill, existing on autopilot in a state of limbo. But now he knew exactly what he wanted, how he wanted his future to be, and was filled with a sense of coming home that he'd never experienced before. To Ben, everything now made sense.

**

Eva chewed her nail and looked out of the window. There was still no sign of Jamie and Hamish. How long had they been? She'd lost track of time but it felt like ages. She turned from the window telling herself not to panic, they would be home soon.

At least both her guests were now settled in their rooms, Dr Hargreaves appearing placated with the food she had provided. In the kitchen she busied herself wiping down already clean surfaces and needlessly moving things about. All she wanted was Jamie and Hamish to come home so they could all be tucked up safely. Not only was she sure she had a nasty cold, but her cut finger was throbbing with pain as well.

She paced back to the window and looked out again, a horrible feeling growing in the pit of her stomach. She hadn't realized how heavy the rain was or how strong the wind had become. What had she been thinking asking Jamie to go out in this? She had only meant for him to take Hamish along the street for a few minutes. Where were they?

She took a deep breath, willing herself to be calm. But no matter how much she tried to convince herself, she knew they should be home by now. Ben's driveway was still empty and his house still in darkness. His absence vexed her but she didn't know why. Part of her longed to rush to him, for him to somehow protect her and make everything all right.

But he didn't owe her any explanations as to his whereabouts. Just because they'd spent the night together didn't mean he was responsible for her and Jamie in any way. It didn't mean he was going to come and rescue her. This was down to her, the way it had always been.

The street was deserted as you'd expect. No sane person would choose to go out on a night like this yet she had actually sent her son out into it. She tried to think where Jamie would go, what he would do. Of course! He'd go to Fraser's house. They'd be there now, engrossed in some game, totally unaware of the time. But even as she dialled the number, she knew Heather would have phoned her if Jamie had turned up at their house. By now the phone was ringing anyway and Douglas answered.

'I don't suppose Jamie's at your house by any chance?' She thought she probably sounded slightly hysterical.

'Heather's at her mother's house and Fraser's upstairs,' Douglas told her.

'Right, of course.' Eva bit her lip.

'Do you want me to come round?' Douglas offered after Eva explained the situation.

'No, no. I'm sure he'll be back any minute.' Eva hung up, her fear now full on. Her heart was pounding and every 'what if' scenario was racing through her mind, none of them good.

For some reason the memory of one Halloween came to her when she had been a small girl. She'd been 'trick or treating' with Sarah and someone dressed up as a ghost had jumped out at them, the deathly image terrifying Eva. She had run back to the house and thrown herself into her father's arms. For those few moments she had felt utterly safe and protected. The memory of her dad holding her and a longing to feel that comfort again was so great it took her breath away. Eva suddenly felt very alone.

***

Ben pulled up in the driveway and instantly knew something was wrong. He saw Eva's shape illuminated in her doorway, looking like she was about to go out and even from a distance he could tell she was agitated, her body tense. He climbed out of the car and ran over to her.

'Eva?'

She turned to him, her beautiful face a picture of anguish. 'I don't know where Jamie is,' she sobbed.

'What do you mean?'

She wiped her hand across her face. 'The guests arrived earlier. One of them was a bit difficult with Hamish so I asked Jamie to take him out for a walk.' She paused, fighting to contain herself. 'I only meant him to be ten minutes. I didn't notice how bad the weather was otherwise I wouldn't have asked him. He hasn't come back. What if he went to the beach? What if Hamish went down to the water? Oh God –' She ran a hand distractedly over her face.

'How long have they been gone?'

'Almost an hour I think … I just know he wouldn't take that long unless something had happened. I'm going out to look for them.'

Ben placed his hands gently on the top of her shoulders forcing her to look at him.

'Listen to me. They'll be all right. Jamie's a sensible boy.' He hoped his reassurance would somehow infiltrate her panic. The look of fear on her face was almost destroying him.

'I have to go and find him,' she said determinedly, starting to move away from him.

'Eva, what if he comes back and you're not here? You have to stay here and let me go. Have you any idea where they might walk?'

Eva ran a hand frantically through her hair. 'Not really – I thought they'd go to the end of the street and back.'

Ben took a step closer to her, took her hand in his. 'It's going to be okay. I'll bring them back.' Eva looked at him with huge eyes, and nodded mutely.

Ben pulled up his hood against the rain and headed straight to the beach. Despite reassuring Eva, he didn't like the idea of Jamie being out in this and the water was his biggest fear. Within seconds he was drenched and as he approached the beach he could see the wind whipping at the water's edge and thought how easy it would be to become disorientated in this weather.

Wherever he was, he hoped Jamie wasn't frightened. Images flashed into his mind of the time he'd got lost on holiday and he hated to think of Eva now and how frantic she must be. He continued to walk along the water's edge scouring the wet sand for footprints, the wind buffeting against his body.

He walked the full length of beach shouting out Jamie's name, then Hamish's, but the wind snatched his voice away. By the time he reached an outcrop of rocks at the end of the beach there was still no sign of them and he started back the way he'd come, this time keeping in close to the shelter of the dunes.

After a few minutes, he stopped dead in his tracks, listening to a noise. Barking. He kept walking, following the sound as it became louder and suddenly, out of the darkness, Hamish appeared. Behind him, looking small and exhausted, was Jamie.

'Jamie!' Ben raced towards them and bent down to him, holding him by the shoulders. 'Are you all right?'

'I – I'm okay.' His voice sounded small. 'Is Mum angry?'

'Of course she's not. She's worried sick but she's going to be so happy to see you. Come on, let's get you home.'

***

'I can see them! Ben's coming with Jamie and Hamish,' Heather called from the window where she'd been looking out while Eva paced up and down. She had come straight from her mother's house after Douglas had relayed Eva's phone call to her.

'Look – they're here.'

Eva joined her at the window, hardly daring to believe Jamie was coming home. Relief flooded her body, every fibre of her being thankful to see her son. She cried out as he came through the door. Ben and Hamish following behind, all of them looking miserable and soaked to the skin.

'Oh, Jamie! Are you all right? I'm so sorry – I should never have asked you to go out.'

'I'm sorry, Mum.' His voice wobbled for a moment before he gave her a small smile. 'I'm fine, honest. Just a bit wet and cold,' he tried to reassure her through chattering teeth. Eva wrapped her arms around him and held him close, breathing him in. He was safe. She pulled away from him, watching him closely.

'What happened? Where did you go?'

'You looked kind of angry so I thought I better take Hamish for a long walk. We went all the way up North Street and then along Market Street ...'

Eva bit her lip as she listened.

'Then we came back down towards the beach. My hands were like really cold and wet and the lead just kind of slipped. Hamish ran off and I just couldn't get him back. Every time I got near him, he kept running off. I think he thought it was a game. I managed to get hold of him at the dunes and that's where Ben found us.'

'Oh, Jamie.' Eva put her hand over her mouth, half laughing, half crying.

'Are you angry with Hamish?' Jamie asked uncertainly.

She looked at the dog who let out a little whimper and she realized how relieved she was to see him too. In that moment she knew he was part of their family.

'No, of course not,' she reassured Jamie giving Hamish a cuddle.

Heather had swung into full maternal mode and had miraculously appeared with towels and hot chocolate for Jamie. Eva realized Ben and Heather hadn't actually met yet and Heather was now introducing herself to him, unashamedly giving him the once-over. She turned to Eva, mouthing 'Oh my God!' before switching her attention to Jamie.

'Right, a hot shower for you, young man. And don't look at me like that. I'll leave you to it, don't worry.'

Eva glanced over to where Ben was rubbing a towel over his hair, his eyes fixed on her. His breathing was heavy, his hair and clothes were damp, and even though she could hardly think straight, some part of her registered how wantonly gorgeous he looked. 'Thank you for bringing Jamie home.' She hated that her voice sounded so remote but she couldn't help it.

'Are you all right?' he asked.

She nodded but wasn't sure at all. Her head seemed to be full of nightmare images of Jamie and water and her whole body was feeling weak, her eyes unable to focus properly. She blinked a few times, reaching out to try and steady herself before suddenly everything went black.

'Whoa there.' She heard Ben's deep voice, vaguely aware of his arms reaching to catch her just as her legs gave way.

A few moments later Ben's face came into focus. She was surprised to find herself sitting on the floor, Ben beside her. She shook her head.

'Oh God, what happened?'

'It's okay – just take it easy. You fainted, but only for a second.'

Eva remained on the floor, feeling herself supported by one of Ben's legs as he crouched beside her. He was studying her, concern etched on his face. 'Eva, what happened to your finger?'

211

'What? Oh, I cut it earlier,' she mumbled vaguely. Ben exchanged a look with Heather.

'Can I take a look at it?' Ben gently unwound the dressing she'd applied earlier and she saw him flinch as he examined her finger. 'That's going to need a couple of stitches. I'm taking you to hospital.'

Eva shook her head, which only made her feel more dizzy. 'No way, I'm fine. I've just got a cold. I'm not leaving Jamie ... or the guests.' Eva attempted to stand but her legs had other ideas. Jamie came over and sat beside her.

'I'm fine, Mum, honest. You look a lot worse than me.'

'Thanks.' Eva turned to him with a watery smile.

'I think what he's trying to say is you need a bit of looking after yourself,' Heather told her. 'I'll stay here and get Jamie sorted and then I'm going to stay the night.'

'You can't do that,' Eva protested.

'I've already arranged everything with Douglas. I'll look after Jamie and be here for the guests if they need anything. I'll take the third guest room – it'll be like a mini-break for me.' She smiled but her expression left no room for disagreement.

'Jamie, will you be okay? I won't be long.' Eva's eyes rested on her son.

'Don't worry about me, Mum.' He came over looking a bit sheepish and cuddled into her.

'I must look bad to get a hug,' she joked feebly.

Heather ushered Jamie upstairs as Ben helped Eva with her jacket. She was aware how tender he was being but somehow that made her feel worse. She longed to let him wrap his arms around her but something stopped her and she felt herself tense as his arm guided her out to the car.

The drive to the hospital took longer because of the rain. Eva glanced over to Ben, his hands gripping the wheel as he concentrated on driving. His jaw was shadowed by stubble and he looked tired. Eva didn't know why Ben had gone to London but it didn't seem to matter any more. She surrendered herself to the warmth and comfort of the car, almost disappointed when they finally arrived at the hospital car park. Ben swung the car into a space, pulling hard on the handbrake.

The rain still fell as they crossed the tarmac and walked through the sliding doors into the brightly lit, sterile world of the hospital. Eva gave her details to the receptionist and they made their way to the waiting room. As Eva sat on one of the plastic chairs Ben went over to the drinks machine and dug in his pocket for change. He brought over a polystyrene cup and handed it to Eva.

'Try and drink this – it's sweet tea.'

'Thanks.'

He sat down close beside her and Eva fought the urge to lean in to him. Longing and apprehension fought within her and fear won.

'Are you okay?' he asked, taking her hand in his.

She nodded. 'Just a bit groggy.'

'Sounds like you've had an eventful few days.'

'Yeah, you could say that.' The morning she'd woken with him now felt like a lifetime away. 'I'm sorry ... for all of this.' She waved a hand distractedly in the air.

He frowned. 'You don't need to apologize, Eva.' They both stared absently at the television screen mounted on the wall, and Eva felt restless, impatient to get home.

'I hope this doesn't take long. I need to get back for Jamie and the guests.'

'Try to relax. Heather's with Jamie and I'm here for you. I can help you with anything –'

'I don't need anyone's help.' Her words sounded harsher than she meant but his concern was confusing her, making her feel defensive. 'I'm sorry – I just mean I can manage on my own.' Ben turned to her, his hand tightening over hers.

'You got my text? I didn't have time to contact you again –'

'You don't have to tell me your movements,' she said, ignoring the hurt look in his eyes. Despite everything she felt for Ben, right now she felt vulnerable and hated it. Not knowing where Jamie had been had brought so many fears to the surface. She was tired and her finger throbbed. 'I'm sorry, I … I'm tired, that's all,' she apologized just as a nurse appeared and called her name.

Chapter Fourteen

'Well, that was hard work,' puffed Heather, collapsing dramatically onto Ben's leather sofa. 'I thought for a moment there, we weren't going to do it.'

'I'm not sure how we did but thanks for helping me.' Eva was perched on the opposite sofa, catching her breath. Somehow, they had managed to lift Ben's two sofas from the hall, angling them back and forth through the doorway until finally they were back in the living room. The process had involved a fair amount of sweating and swearing.

'How's your finger now?'

Eva held it up. 'Dissolving. Well, the stitches are anyway.' Eva had been given two stitches at the hospital and Ben had driven her home, a horrible silence settling over them. In one way there was so much to say but the air between them felt so tense, neither of them seemed capable of finding the right thing to say. Ben had driven with a grim determination as if sensing Eva's need to get home to Jamie. She had thanked him and said goodnight and found Heather waiting for her.

Eva had gone straight to see Jamie and had sat watching him sleeping until she could hardly keep her own eyes open. After a good night's sleep and a couple of strong painkillers Eva was feeling better by the next morning and well enough to attend to her guests. Everything had gone smoothly with their stay and they had checked out on Wednesday morning seemingly none the wiser to the drama that had unfolded on Monday night. Even Dr Hargreaves bid farewell with a smile.

'Is Jamie okay after his ordeal?' Heather asked now.

'He's right as rain – you know what kids are like. I don't know what I would have done without you that night.'

'It wasn't only me.' Heather shot her a meaningful look, which Eva ignored. 'Have you seen Ben?'

'Er, not since that night,' Eva answered lightly.

'I hope you're not avoiding him.'

'Why would I do that?'

'You tell me. I sense you're holding back in some way and I can only imagine what's going on inside that head of yours.'

'I've been busy, that's all. I wanted to get this room finished.'

Heather stood up casting her a sceptical look. 'And it looks wonderful, it really does, but you should speak to him. And soon.'

'I will.'

'Good because he really is heavenly,' Heather gushed. 'Did you see the way he looked at you?'

Eva smiled despite herself. 'An incurable romantic, aren't you?'

'All the time I've known you, you've worked so hard, Eva. I just think it's time you did something for yourself. It is all right for you to have a life you know,' Heather said picking up her bag. 'Talk to him, that's all I'm saying. Now, I need to go and collect some children from somewhere.'

Eva shook her head in wonder. 'I don't know how you keep track.'

Eva waved Heather off and Ben's house fell silent. Eva was alone with her thoughts. Did she have a chance of real happiness? She didn't think so, because now she knew there could be no future for her and Ben.

She'd had a terrible, sleepless night thinking until her head hurt. The conclusion she had reached, sometime around three in the morning, wasn't one she was happy with but she saw no other way. Her body might want Ben but she'd been unable to reconcile her physical longing with her jumbled thoughts.

She picked up a cloth and spray and started to give the windows a good clean, finding herself mulling over everything again.

Although no harm had come to Jamie, Eva had felt genuine fear for the time he was missing. All the years she had coped, dealing with all the highs and lows of bringing up a child on her own but, in that moment when fear had gripped her, she had wanted to run to Ben. Instinctively she had wanted to go to him and for him to somehow make it better. She had felt unable to cope – and admitting she needed Ben wasn't something that sat comfortably with her; in fact it terrified her.

She thought of the life she had with Jamie. He was the single most important thing in her life. She knew in some ways she had created a bubble for her and Jamie, a place where she felt safe. That had meant keeping Jamie close, focusing on her business and now she realized it also meant not letting anyone in because she never wanted to rely on someone who might not always be there. She didn't have the luxury of making a mistake, not when she had her son to look after.

She had let Ben infiltrate her safe nest, imagined what life could be like with him, little scenarios playing out in her head. Family occasions, school concerts, and sports days – all those things she had got through by herself. She had let herself get carried away.

Eva shook her head, rubbing hard at a streak that had appeared on the window, feeling angry with herself. She had put herself before Jamie. For those few hours she hadn't made him her priority and now she was paying the price. Somehow she had lost control of things – feeling unwell, cutting her finger, putting Jamie in danger. The sequence of events all led back to her letting Ben in.

Things had moved too fast. She had given in to her desire too quickly and guilt was eating her up from the inside. Being with Ben had affected her judgement and she had let her guard down. But now she knew what she had to do. She needed to go back to the life she had before Ben.

She stood back, content to see the windows now gleaming, and then pulled out her phone to check the time. Jamie had football after school so there was no rush. She took a long look around the room. With the sofas now in place, the room was finished and she hoped with all her heart Ben liked it.

The room had changed beyond recognition since the MacKenzies lived here and Eva hoped it would be filled with life and happiness again one day. Like all families they'd had their ups and downs but they'd been strong and loving and always there for each other. And wasn't that what everyone wanted after all? It was certainly all she had ever wanted.

She wasn't surprised when she heard the key in the door. Maybe in some ways she'd been hoping for Ben to come home so they could have the conversation she knew they had to have. Ignoring her pounding heart she told herself she was doing the right thing. She squared her shoulders, attempting a brightness she didn't feel, and by the time Ben appeared at the living room door, her smile was in place.

***

Ben guessed Eva had been avoiding him. He understood how difficult it had been for her the night Jamie went missing and had instinctively given her space and time to work things through in her own mind. Today he couldn't wait any longer; he had to see her. Her hair was held up messily with a clasp and she was wearing her dungarees that he loved so much. She greeted him with a smile but wouldn't meet his eyes and his heart sank.

'So, do you like it?' she asked in an overbright voice, her arm sweeping around the room. Ben hadn't stepped in the room for days even though he'd known she was close to finishing. Now he was staggered by the transformation, amazed how it had changed from an empty, lifeless space into a beautiful room. She had even managed to make his cold austere furniture look right somehow. Every detail had been thought of from the newly varnished floorboards to the freshly painted cornicing detail.

For a moment he was lost for words. He knew how much effort this must have taken and she had done it for him. And yet the tension from her was tangible and he knew this moment wasn't how either of them imagined it was going to be.

'It's incredible. I can hardly believe you did all this by yourself.'

She at least managed a small smile in response but still avoided his gaze. 'Do you like the colours?'

'They're great.'

'I wanted something neutral but not wishy-washy. So I chose this mid-tone browny grey, which warms up the room and makes it feel cosy.' She was talking quickly, moving around the room. 'I painted it right to the ceiling to give the room height and you'll see I did the woodwork a paler shade but in the same palette. I think white would have been too stark.'

Ben nodded as she continued, watching her closely.

'I've put a rug down, with touches of blue in it, and I made you a floating shelf in the recess so you can put some of your books on it ...'

'Eva, stop.'

She turned, finally looking at him. 'What is it?'

'The room is lovely. Truly, it's amazing what you've done. Thank you.'

'You're welcome.' She looked down, tucking a strand of hair behind her ear.

'Can we talk now?'

'Um, sure.'

'I want to tell you why I went away.'

'I've said already, you don't need to.'

'I do. Please – sit with me.' He took hold of her hand and gently pulled her down beside him on the sofa, keeping hold of her hand. 'I went back to my house near London, where I grew up.'

'I didn't know you still had another home.'

'I hadn't told you about it – but only because it's something I haven't wanted to deal with.' She met his eyes with a quizzical look.

'After my mother moved into the care home, I didn't know what to do with the house. After a while I rented it out –'

'Really, you don't have to explain ...'

'Please, Eva. Just hear me out. The tenants renting the house moved out so it's been lying empty. I got a phone call to say the house had been broken into.' He glanced down at Eva's hand, took a deep breath.

'The day I took my mother out of the house for the last time was the hardest day I've ever had to go through. I haven't been back to the house for years – I haven't been able to face it. But when I got the phone call I knew I had to deal with it. And I knew I could face it because of you.'

A small crease appeared on her forehead. 'Why because of me?'

'Because of the way you make me feel – like I could face anything.'

Eva stared at him for a moment then dropped her gaze, letting him continue.

'When I came here, I wasn't sure about anything any more. Arriving without Samantha I thought ... I thought I'd be devastated. It didn't take me long to work out what we had wasn't much – just a mutually convenient relationship. The last thing I expected was to meet someone who could make me feel like you do. At first I didn't know how to handle it. I couldn't believe I could fall in love so quickly. But with you, everything feels right. You're beautiful, caring, and strong – you make me happy. We haven't known each other long but the time we've had together has meant more to me than I've ever known with anyone else. I'm so in love with you, Eva.'

Eva's head was down and Ben couldn't see her face and after a moment she slipped her hand out of his. She stood up and took a few steps away from him, creating a space between them. With her eyes still lowered to the floor she shook her head slightly.

'I can't do this – you and me. It's too difficult,' she said eventually.

Ben rose from the sofa and walked over to her. 'Difficult how?'

'I'm not saying I don't have feelings for you because I do. What happened between us has been amazing – the night we had was amazing. But don't you see? I put myself first and changed things. When Jamie went missing it was because I let my guard down.'

Ben frowned. 'Bad things happen, Eva. You can't control everything.'

She shook her head, a strand of hair falling from her clasp. 'That moment I thought something terrible had happened, I was on my own. I've learnt to be self-reliant and I can't change that now. Maybe I over-reacted when I didn't know where Jamie was but that's what you do when you're alone. It's down to me. Not anyone else.'

'Eva, I can only imagine how hard it's been for you on your own. But I think we have something special –'

'Maybe we do, but I can't take that risk. Do you know how frightened I was after Paul died? When I didn't know where Jamie was I felt that fear again – I won't put myself in that position again.'

'How do you think Jamie would feel knowing you sacrificed your own happiness for him?'

She rounded on him, her eyes flashing with anger. 'Don't you dare bring him into this!'

Ben stepped back, holding his hands up in surrender. 'I'm sorry – I would never tell you how to bring up your son.' He ran a hand through his hair and when he spoke his voice was low and gentle. 'You do an incredible job, Eva, and I respect that. I was only trying to make the point it's impossible for you to protect him all the time. Life is full of risks but those risks are how he will learn and make him the man he will become. I'll never be Jamie's father but I can care. You and Jamie are a family and it would mean everything to me to be part of that family, Eva. Would you give us that chance – to be a family?'

Ben tensed, waiting for her to say something. She was looking at him and her eyes glistened with unshed tears. She took a breath as if composing herself and gave him a sad smile.

'I'm sorry, Ben. I … I can't commit to us. I need things to stay as they are.' She lifted her hand and tenderly brushed his cheek and then turned and left. Ben stood, fists clenched by his sides, staring at the front door as if willing it to open and for Eva to walk back in.

As he turned, something caught his eye on the mantelpiece that he hadn't noticed before. Beautifully mounted in a silver gilt frame was a photograph of

Ben and his parents on the beach. It must have been taken the year before his dad died, their last family holiday. He hadn't seen the photo for years but it had been one of the few things he had taken from his mother's house. Eva must have found it in the box he had given her.

He stood motionless, staring at it. He could hardly bring himself to touch it and when he did, his hand was shaking. Knowing Eva had done this for him just made seeing her walk out a whole lot more difficult. Ben knew he had fallen deeply in love with Eva but hadn't managed to find a way of telling her without frightening her.

He could see how hard she had worked to get the life she had and the last thing he wanted was to come and mess it up for her. He shook his head in frustration, not knowing how he could carry on living here and not be with her.

Chapter Fifteen

Eva sipped a glass of hot water and lemon, reminding herself it was supposed to be good for her. What had that article said? Rejuvenating, cleansing, healing. She definitely needed some of that. She tried not to think of her usual silky-smooth morning coffee. Things that tasted delicious weren't necessarily good for you she thought savagely, enduring a few more sips before sloshing the rest down the sink. Next was a vitamin pill, anything to try to make her feel better.

Although not usually inclined to spend much time in front of a mirror, this morning Eva had studied her reflection and it hadn't made for happy viewing. How had she managed to go from glowing to drab in such a short space of time? she wondered bleakly. Everything about her looked and felt dull. Her body felt as if it had gone into some sort of meltdown the past few days.

At night she was unable to sleep, her body restless and her mind racing. During the day she tried to keep busy, finding anything to keep herself occupied. Cupboards were sorted, drawers emptied, floors scrubbed but still she couldn't banish thoughts of Ben from her mind. She knew she had made the right decision, so why then did it feel so bad?

She told herself it was all about looking forward. Making a few plans, focusing on other things – such as becoming pet-friendly. She'd been doing some reading and researching. The good news was that allowing dogs would certainly open up a new market and potentially generate more income. Families took their dogs on holiday and not many other guest houses in the area allowed pets so that would give her an advantage.

But there were plenty of issues to consider – she'd need to think about insurance, possible damage to property, and she'd have to provide food, bowls, and towels. And the house would have to be kept meticulously clean in case of dog hairs. She'd revisited the idea of opening in winter and had even found herself speculating exactly what Greg Ritchie's 'investment opportunities' were.

In the hall she called up to Jamie as she wrapped a scarf around her neck. Maybe she could do more decorating, she thought, put an advert in the local paper. But they were all just ideas, thoughts going nowhere. Eva felt as if reality had shifted in some way and now she wasn't sure what she wanted any more. Time and time again she reminded herself she'd managed just fine before Ben and she could do it again.

'I'm ready, Mum.' Jamie's voice broke into her thoughts and she turned to him with a bright smile.

'Good. I'll just get Hamish sorted in his basket. We won't be too long.'

It was the first day of the school Christmas holiday and having persuaded Jamie a visit to Edinburgh's natural history museum would be useful for his project on ancient Egypt next term, Eva had arranged to meet Sarah and her mother in the museum café. Eva had talked with Sarah on the phone and exchanged a few texts, glad they were slowly returning to how they used to be.

Eva locked the front door listening to Jamie mutter mutinously that he'd better not see anyone he knew at the museum. Eva turned and spotted Ben bundling a holdall into the boot of his car. She kept her head down, feeling pathetic for doing so. She would learn to block the feelings, to deal with seeing him – they were neighbours after all – she just wasn't quite there yet. Oh God, now he was coming over to them.

'How're you doing, Jamie?' Ben waved to Jamie who was settling himself in the front seat.

'Yeah, good.' Jamie smiled back.

'These are for you,' Ben said to Jamie handing him a boxed set of *Star War* films. 'All the original ones. I know how hard you've been working on your maths and thought you could give yourself a treat and watch these over the holidays.'

'Brilliant, thanks, Ben!'

He switched his gaze to Eva who was standing by the open car door, frozen to the spot. 'Hi, Eva. How are you?'

He looked tired and unshaven and so gorgeous that Eva felt her body betray her and she inhaled sharply.

'Great, yes … fine.' She'd been aiming for casual and confident but somehow her voice came out weirdly high.

'I wanted to check you still have a set of keys for my house?'

'Oh, yes. Sorry, I should have given them back to you.'

'No, it's fine. I'm heading down south for a bit – I don't want to leave the house in London empty over the holidays.' He ran a hand along his jagged jawline, looking distracted. 'Would you mind holding on to them – just in case something happens while I'm away?'

'Oh, yes … of course.'

'I know you're more than capable of handling anything.' A ghost of a smile appeared on his lips. 'Take care of yourself, Eva.'

'You too.'

She took a deep breath and climbed into the car. Just because he looked tired didn't mean she should worry about him making that long journey. He would be fine, she told herself, glancing at the clock on the dashboard and pulling out of the driveway.

They had plenty of time so she decided to take the coastal road, driving through the pretty fishing villages of Crail and Anstruther while Christmas songs played on the radio. They had just driven over the Forth Road Bridge when Jamie surprised her.

'You know, Mum, I really like Ben.'

Her hands tightened on the wheel but she kept her voice casual. 'He's been a great help with your maths.'

'And he's taught me how to move all the pieces on a chess board.'

'That's good,' Eva replied evenly.

'I liked when he came to our house. When's he going to come for dinner again?'

Eva swallowed. 'Oh, I'm not sure. He's probably busy at the university.'

'But I can still go and ask him stuff?'

'Of course, I'm sure he wouldn't mind that.' Eva frowned, wondering if Jamie had picked up on anything.

'We've started algebra at school,' he told her sounding miserable.

'Well, don't worry. I can always help you.'

He made a face, looking doubtful.

'What? We'll be able to work it out between us.'

'Mum, you can't google it. I need someone to, like, actually explain it properly. It's good when Ben helps – I just sort of understand it more.'

In all her own turmoil she hadn't stopped to think just how much Jamie and Ben had connected. She had been trying to protect Jamie and didn't feel good about her son missing Ben. Jamie clearly loved having Ben in their lives and she couldn't deny he'd been a great role model for her son. She felt her shoulders slump, dismayed that trying to do the right thing seemed so wrong at times.

When they arrived in Edinburgh, parking was a bit of a nightmare but eventually Eva found a space on the outskirts of the centre. They got to Princes Street twenty minutes later, Eva enjoying the views of the castle and the bustling Christmas shoppers while Jamie complained about the distance they had to walk. Entering the museum they passed through the grand central hall, Eva pointing to portraits of famous Scottish doctors while Jamie showed more interest in the stuffed animals and dinosaur skeleton. They found Sarah and Helen already seated at a table in the café.

'Hi, Mum.' Eva bent and kissed her powdery cheek and eyed Jamie to do the same. Eva slipped off her coat and scarf, giving Sarah a double take. Her clothes were still very Sarah-esque but she wore pretty pearl drop earrings and looked softer somehow. She stood to embrace Eva and turned to Jamie.

'Would you like to come and help me get the drinks?' she asked him sounding a tad awkward.

'Er, yeah,' Jamie responded.

The role of aunt wasn't one Sarah slipped into naturally but Eva could see she was trying and appreciated the effort.

'Mum, usual for you?'

'Yes please, darling.'

'Eva?'

'I'll have a cappuccino please,' Eva answered, all intentions for a decaf-skinny abandoned. She smiled across at her mother who she felt scrutinize her.

'How are you, darling?' Helen asked.

'I'm fine, Mum.'

'You look a bit … peaky.'

Eva straightened herself and smoothed down her hair as if that would make a difference but for once couldn't argue with her mother's appraisal.

'I'm all right – had a couple of bad night sleeps, that's all.'

Tilting her head to the side, Helen regarded her.

'You know, there's a wonderful spa I go to. I could book us in for a day after Christmas … we could go together and make a day of it, have a few treatments.' Eva's excuse was on the tip of her tongue but she stopped herself. Thinking of how far she and Sarah had come recently, maybe it was time to try and improve relations with her mum and after all, a few spa treatments might not go amiss.

'That sounds really nice, thanks, Mum.' Eva was rewarded with a beatific smile.

'How is Jamie getting on at school?'

Ignoring what she knew was a reference to his academic progress, Eva deliberately focused instead on what mattered to her.

'He's great. Making plenty of friends, playing sports. He seems to have settled really well at high school.'

'And how's he doing in all his subjects? It's important he makes a good start in first year.'

'Of course, and he's doing fine, Mum,' Eva reassured her. It had been a bittersweet moment when Jamie had come home proudly declaring his mark to be one of the highest in the class maths test. Clearly Ben was a good teacher but then that didn't surprise Eva. She looked over at Jamie now standing in the queue with Sarah, something he said making her laugh. Eva returned her focus back to Helen. Unlike her own pallor, her mother's appearance held an undeniable radiance that Eva assumed was thanks to George.

Sarah and Eva had talked on the phone, Sarah explaining that she and Helen had discussed their 'new situation' as she described it. Eva hadn't asked for the details, feeling it was between Sarah and her mother. As long as they were both happy, that was enough for her. Sarah had made the decision to go to Holland in the New Year for a couple of weeks to see how things went and Eva was thrilled for her and hoped it all worked out with Jon.

'Sarah told me she's going to Holland in the New Year,' she mentioned now.

Helen nodded graciously, as if she was giving the idea her blessing. 'I think it's the right thing for her to do and I'm sure it will all work out the way it's meant to.'

'And you? You'll be all right here without her? You know that I can come and help you with anything or you could come to St Andrews.'

'I know, darling. Thank you but I'll be fine.' A faint blush rose in her cheeks. 'You know about … George?'

'Yes. And I'm happy for you, Mum.'

Her mother smiled, managing to look demure but slightly uncomfortable at the same time. 'I wondered if you and Jamie might like to meet him over Christmas – if that would be all right with you?'

Eva nodded. 'Sure, that's a good idea.'

'Oh and another thing.' Helen paused. 'I haven't chosen my kitchen tiles yet and was hoping that maybe you could help me choose?'

'Of course! I'd be really happy to do that with you, Mum.' This was a day for surprises.

'Sarah told me how lovely your house is looking and I know you've always had a good eye for colour and design.' Coming from her mother, that was tantamount to high praise and Eva smiled at her just as Jamie arrived with a tray, everything on it almost sliding off in his hurry to get to the table.

'Mum! Guess what?' Eva grabbed the tray just in time. 'Aunt Sarah said she would take me to a rugby match at Murrayfield.'

'Really? Wow, that's great.'

'Is that all right with you, Eva?' Sarah checked passing the drinks along.

'Of course, Jamie will love that,' Eva replied gratefully.

Helen poured tea from a little cream teapot and looked at her grandson. 'So, how was your activity weekend, Jamie? Did you have fun?'

'Awesome. There's photos I can show you.'

'You didn't tell me that, Jamie.' Eva looked at him in surprise.

Jamie shrugged. 'They're up on the website now – can I use your phone, Aunt Sarah?'

'Sure,' she replied, digging in her bag.

After a few minutes Jamie had called up the website and was providing a running commentary as his finger swiped over the screen. 'That was the day we did mountain biking – we got to go along these tracks in the forest ...'

Eva sipped her coffee watching Jamie recount his experiences. He passed the phone to Eva after he'd finished so she could look at them properly. At first it was odd seeing the evidence of an experience he'd had without her, to know that he would have those memories that didn't include her.

She zoomed in on a photo of Jamie, rope coiled around his body and his face just visible under his helmet as he prepared to descend a rock face. Eva blinked, an unfamiliar feeling coming over her as she studied the photo of Jamie about to do something dangerous. Instead of reacting with fear, she felt overwhelmingly proud of him.

Wasn't it wonderful that he was so confident? That he wasn't afraid? He'd done it all by himself and had coped on his own without her being there. This was just his first school trip – imagine all the other things he still had to experience. She scrolled through more photos, seeing all the children's faces shining with excitement and a sense of achievement. They were children being children and not scared by life.

Her role as a mother was to protect him, not to hold him back. Life involved opportunities and risks but that was how he would learn. And in that instant Eva knew she had to accept and embrace change. She had to let Jamie live his life and not pass her own fears on to him. Eva swallowed down the lump that had formed in her throat, wondering just how she had let herself become so afraid.

Eva looked over to see her mother looking fondly at Jamie. She was smiling at something he said and as she very precisely placed her cup on its saucer, her gaze caught Eva's. Eva recognized a softness in her mother's eyes, one she hadn't noticed before, and in that moment Eva knew whatever else, her mother loved her. They hadn't always shared the same outlook on life but if Eva had learnt one thing, it was that there was no easy or perfect way to be a parent. You did the best you could.

Gathering their things, Helen began to list the exhibits they should go and see. Jamie wasn't looking too enthusiastic until pickled body parts were mentioned and then his face lit up. Sarah and Eva fell in step behind their mother and Jamie as they forged ahead, Helen assuming the role of museum guide.

Eva felt Sarah's eyes on her. 'Are you all right?' she asked.

Eva breathed in deeply, not trusting herself to speak for a moment. Something about the warmth of the museum, the families milling about, and the anticipation of Christmas made her feel disconcerted in some way. She cleared her throat.

'Of course I'm fine. Why?' she said with a weak laugh.

'You just seem a bit quiet – not yourself. Jamie's okay, isn't he?'

Something about Sarah's expression took Eva back to the summer when she had been sixteen and madly in love with Danny Collins. Convinced he was about to ask her out, she'd been devastated when he'd started going out instead with Linda Dodds. It had been Sarah who'd told Eva he wasn't worth it, taking her shopping and telling her everyone knew Linda Dodds was easy anyway. Eva regarded Sarah now, remembering how lucky she'd felt all those years ago to have such a brilliant big sister, and was suddenly overcome by the need to confide.

'It's not Jamie. It's me.'

Sarah stopped in her tracks. 'You're not sick are you?'

A rueful laugh came from Eva. 'I suppose some people might think love is a sickness.'

Sarah's eyes searched her face. 'You're in love?'

'It would appear so.'

'Who with?'

Keeping half an eye on Jamie and Helen who were up ahead studying the bronze figure of an

Egyptian god, Eva recounted the past few weeks to Sarah including telling Ben nothing could happen between them because she had to focus on Jamie. Sarah had listened carefully and then stopped, turning to Eva.

'You know, I've done a lot of thinking in the past few weeks and it's only now I truly understand the impact Dad's death had on us. Just at the time we were both finding out who we were we had to deal with losing him and Mum being on her own. I was happy staying near Mum but I've realized I was using her as an excuse not to move forward with my life. I was scared of things going wrong with Jon so it was easier to say to myself I needed to stay with Mum.'

'And then Mum started going out with George.'

'Exactly, and then it became harder to use her as a reason not to be with Jon.'

'It was you who told me, Eva, do you remember? A chance of happiness is too precious to throw away. And you were right. If you love Ben, if you think this might be the real thing, you can't ignore it for all the wrong reasons.'

'The wrong reasons?'

Sarah put a hand on her arm and spoke gently. 'Do you think you might be using Jamie the way I used Mum – to shield you from Ben in case you get hurt?'

Eva opened her mouth to deny it and then closed it again. 'I don't know, maybe,' she sighed. 'Oh God he's so great and I've totally blown it.'

'You don't know that,' Sarah told her with a smile. 'It sounds like you might have something special but you won't know until you take that chance will you? And you deserve it, Eva.'

Eva just about managed to swallow down the lump that had formed in her throat.

'So do you.'

They remained in thoughtful silence as they started to make their way towards Jamie who was waving them over to see something.

Eva could see life was changing for her sister and her mother, both hopefully on their way to finding happiness and love. And of course Eva wanted that too. She heard Sarah's words in her head and deep down knew she was right. She was using Jamie as an excuse not to be with Ben when in actual fact if anything he was a reason for them to be together. The thought of Ben driving to London on his own suddenly filled her with regret and she hoped she hadn't made a huge mistake. She prayed with all her heart it wasn't too late for her.

Chapter Sixteen

'Have a good day!' Eva called after Jamie who was looking slightly subdued and bleary-eyed as he trudged over to his friends, ready to go to school. 'Come on, Hamish,' Eva sighed heading in the opposite direction to the beach. Jamie hadn't looked too impressed when she'd woken him this morning, not that Eva could blame him. First day back at school in January wasn't something most children would relish but at least she knew he'd had a good holiday.

Christmas had been spent in Edinburgh and Jamie and Eva had been introduced to George. Eva had taken to him immediately. A widower, he was friendly, relaxed, and at pains to show he wasn't trying to bulldoze his way into their family. Fortunately for Hamish, he was also dog lover, which helped sway Helen into allowing Hamish into the house. Christmas at her mother's house was never going to be a noisy, chaotic family affair but it was all reassuringly familiar. The decorations were stylish but sparse, the beautifully wrapped presents were handed out one by one, and the dinner was traditional but rather formal.

After their meal, Eva had made the coffee with Helen in the kitchen, agreeing a date to go tile shopping while Jamie played Monopoly with Sarah and George. Jamie's holiday had been a whirl of activity, Eva taxiing him about to friends' houses or trips to the cinema. She'd found herself with a free afternoon after depositing Jamie and some friends at a paintballing party. She'd driven to the shops intent on some rare retail therapy but ended up wandering aimlessly, the crowds only making her feel more alone.

New Year's Eve had been spent at Heather's, which definitely was a noisy and chaotic family affair. Eva had taken her phone out to the garden before midnight to speak to Sarah, raising a glass to her over the phone. She was flying to Holland the next afternoon to meet Jon and Eva had gulped back tears of happiness for her sister.

Eva had looked up to the sky to see if she could make out the constellation Ben had shown her but her tears were falling freely and she couldn't see anything. Perhaps it was the unique perspective that New Year's Eve can bring or maybe it was gazing at the night sky wondering if Ben was doing the same, but standing alone in the garden, something provided Eva with a clarity of thinking. She had wiped her eyes, topped up her glass, and rejoined the party knowing what she needed to do.

Eva unhooked Hamish's lead when she reached the beach and watched as he went running off to explore the new scents of the day. She had discovered if she walked him until he was so exhausted he simply didn't have the energy to misbehave. She knew it wasn't exactly a proper training method but it seemed to be working and came with the added advantage of killing time.

They passed one other dog walker and in the distance Eva could see a runner but not many were braving the beach today. January always held a certain bleakness Eva thought and it was reflected perfectly in the weather today. Charcoal swirls of clouds scudded across the sky and the wind from the east was making it bitterly cold. Eva huddled deeper into her jacket. Small waves washed up on the shore and then trickled back into the sea and she laughed at Hamish with his little coat on, staying well away from the water. 'Too cold for you, boy.'

The runner had closed the distance between them and it was Hamish who recognized him first, his tail whipping frantically from side to side as he raced towards Ben. Eva frowned, certain she hadn't seen Ben's car, and she was hardly likely to miss it given that she had been painfully aware of his empty driveway since he had left.

She carried on walking, watching as Ben slowed his pace and stopped to greet Hamish who was squirming with delight. He was kitted out in dark layers for running and a hat pulled down over his ears. His dark gaze fixed on Eva as she approached and she could see his chest moving as he recovered his breathing. The sight of him made her own heart beat wildly and she could quite happily have thrown herself into his arms pretty much the way Hamish was doing now.

'Hi, Eva. How have you been?'

There was a brief smile but uncertainty in his eyes. It was almost like seeing him for the first time again, only now she knew just how much she loved him and the stakes were much higher. She faltered – what if he felt differently now?

'I'm fine, thanks.'

She'd imagined this conversation a hundred times over the past few days. In her head the words had flowed easily but now she felt clumsy, her mouth unable to form the words she needed to say. Instead she cast her eyes down, studying a pretty pink shell lying on the sand.

'How was your Christmas?' he asked, still sounding slightly out of breath from his run.

'Good. Jamie had a great time anyway.' She kept her attention on the shell, scuffing it with the toe of her boot before she looked up at him. 'What about you – how was London?' Eva wondered if that sounded as petulant to Ben as it did to her own ears and thought she saw the tiniest flicker of amusement in his eyes before he replied.

'London was busy and noisy, just as I expected it to be. But I had a few things to do, saw a few old friends – I got back yesterday.'

'I didn't notice your car in the driveway,' she remarked.

'I sold it in London so I got a flight back.' He shrugged. 'It wasn't really me. I thought I might look for something else.'

Eva nodded mutely just as a huge black cloud suddenly stole all the light and she felt a sudden chill.

'I'd better call Hamish back.' She tried to sound confident but knew there was every chance Hamish would have other ideas. True to form, Hamish totally ignored her and after a couple of failed attempts, Ben offered assistance.

'Would you like me to have a go?'

Eva shrugged. 'Sure.'

Ben placed two fingers in his mouth and gave an ear-splitting whistle. Hamish stopped in his tracks. 'Here, boy!'

Eva watched in disbelief as Hamish trotted over, the very model of obedience, and looked up adoringly at Ben.

'I don't believe it!' Eva rolled her eyes. She clasped the lead to his collar just as a deluge of frozen rock-like hailstones started pelting down from the dark sky.

'We should get back.' They walked in silence, Eva aware of Ben's hand on the small of her back as he guided them away from the beach. By the time they reached the row of houses, Eva's face was stinging with cold and she was shivering although she was sure she couldn't attribute that all to the weather. They came to Ben's house first and Hamish scuttled up his path. Ben turned questioningly to Eva and saw her shaking.

'You're frozen; we'd better get you inside.'

In the hall they shook themselves out and Ben gestured for Eva to go through to the living room while he made something hot to drink. Eva took off her boots, feeling suddenly more relaxed as she walked into the familiar room, almost a sense of belonging enveloping her.

A few brochures sitting on the coffee table caught her attention and she instantly recognized them as estate agent brochures and she felt her heart drop. She skimmed the glossy pages of properties being sold in St Andrews, the clever angles showing the staged interiors to their best advantage. Ben came in carrying two mugs and she turned to him, holding up the brochures with a questioning eyebrow.

'Why do you have these?' she asked, attempting to sound casual, dreading what the answer might be.

'Oh, right. I went to see an estate agent when I came back yesterday – he gave me these.' He handed her a mug and then lit the fire, which cast a warm glow around the room.

'Are – are you thinking of selling?' Eva swallowed.

He shrugged. 'I thought I should at least do the exercise. If I did sell and look for a smaller place, I wanted to see what was out there and how easy it would be to sell this place.'

Eva bit her lip, taking her mug over to the window, composing herself before turning to face Ben. 'I've heard January isn't a good time to sell.'

Ben's mug stopped halfway to his mouth and he stared at Eva for a moment before his expression changed. 'Really?' he said, continuing with his drink. 'The estate agent seemed to think it was the perfect time to sell.'

'Well he would, wouldn't he? You know what estate agents are like – they always find a way of pitching it. You can't trust them.'

'Is that right?' he mused.

Eva nodded. 'Uh-huh, definitely,' she confirmed. 'And at the very least you should probably get the kitchen done – kitchens really help to sell a house.'

Ben quirked an eyebrow. 'I don't know, that sounds like a lot of work. I'd need to find the right person for the job and I know how difficult that can be.'

Eva felt her heart thumping as she walked across the room to Ben. Slowly she placed her untouched tea down on the table and stood in front of him and looked into his eyes.

'Stay,' she said, her voice almost a whisper. Ben fixed her with a look, his eyes never leaving hers.

'Say that again,' he said quietly.

Feeling suddenly brave she moved closer to him so they were almost touching and tiptoed so that her mouth was close to Ben's ear.

'Stay,' she repeated. 'Stay with me and Jamie and Hamish. I want you to be part of our family, Ben.' He pulled back just enough so his eyes could search her face.

'Last time we spoke you didn't seem to think that was such a good idea.'

'I know. But I got it wrong. I panicked – I can see that now. I've done such a good job of protecting myself, of convincing myself that I can manage on my own, it was difficult to let go of that. But I've had time to think and I don't want to live in fear any more. I can't control every little thing about Jamie's life. I've missed you so much ... I love you so much. I want to take this chance to be happy with you.'

Time seemed to stop as Ben stood silently and Eva could hear her own heart thundering in her chest. 'Aren't you ... going to say anything?' She swallowed.

Ben stared at her for a long moment and then held out his hand. 'Will Hamish be all right here on his own?' he asked, the gruffness in his voice and the expression on his face sending a shock of heat through her body.

Eva glanced at Hamish who she could swear was smiling. 'I think he'll be okay for a little while,' she stammered before taking Ben's hand.

A little while turned into a long while and Hamish was stretched out in a deep sleep in front of the fire when Ben and Eva padded back downstairs hand in hand. Eva ambled over to the window and gazed out to the familiar setting, except that everything looked shiny and new somehow. The dark clouds were starting to drift away and Eva shook her head slightly, thinking of all the stormy weather recently, wondering where it had all come from. But the worst of it seemed to be over, she thought, seeing the patches of blue sky beginning to appear on the horizon.

She turned to look at Ben who was sitting on the sofa watching her. Eva thought he looked how she felt: a bit dazed and deliriously happy. He patted the space beside him and Eva tucked herself in close to Ben, feeling the warmth and strength of his body beside her as he wrapped an arm around her.

'So does that mean you're staying?'

'I'm definitely staying.' He smiled, planting a kiss on the side of her head. Eva sighed happily, letting her body sink further into his arms.

'It's still a big house for one person though,' she mused.

'Yeah, I've been thinking about that.'

'And?'

'And that's where you come in.'

'Oh?'

'I was kind of hoping you'd like to decorate it ...'

Eva swivelled round to face him, her eyes shining. 'I'd love to decorate it! I have a million ideas ...'

'I'm counting on it.' Ben smiled. 'And I was hoping it could become our family home, Eva. For you, me, and Jamie. And Hamish of course.'

'We move in here?'

'Only if you wanted, when you were ready.' His voice sounded tentative now, his beautiful dark eyes studying her face so intently that in that moment Eva knew she trusted Ben totally, knew that he would love and cherish their new family as much as she would. Because that's what they would be, a family. She met his gaze, feeling a rush of happiness.

'I'm ready ... we're ready.' She smiled. There was so much to think about and she paused as she tried to process the thoughts tumbling about her head, the feel of Ben's fingers running through her hair almost making it impossible to think at all.

'You've gone quiet,' Ben said.

'I was thinking about the guest house, how I'd be able to still run it.'

'Well, I've given that some thought too.'

'You have been doing a lot of thinking.' She grinned.

'I wondered … how you'd feel about running your house as self-catering accommodation. That way you'd still have your business but you'd have more time for other projects – you have such a talent for interiors I thought you might be interested in taking an interior design course.'

Eva was beginning to feel wonderfully dizzy, hardly believing Ben had thought of all that for her.

'I've also decided to rent out my old London home again but it's going to need a total makeover, if you were interested. But of course, these are only ideas I've had – it's entirely up to you.' He took her hand and brought it to his mouth, kissing it softly. 'I just want you to be happy, Eva.'

'I am happy and I love all your ideas.' She smiled. 'Sounds like I'm going to be busy then …'

'Not too busy for a honeymoon at some point, I hope?'

Eva felt a joyous smile spread across her mouth, warmth and happiness flooding into her very being. She buried her face in his neck, feeling safe and warm and lovely. She couldn't wait to tell Moira and Donald that she'd be moving in – they would love that as much as she did.

Ben cupped Eva's face in his hands and looked lovingly at her. 'You once said to me home is about knowing you don't want to be anywhere else. For me, home is wherever you are, Eva.'

'In that case,' she said kissing him, 'welcome home.'

Acknowledgements

A huge thank-you to my lovely editor Hannah Smith for her unfailing enthusiasm and expert guidance every step of the way. Also to Helena Newton for her skilful work and to all the team at HQ Digital.

A special thank-you Lynne Morton – for her support, lovely notepads and making sure I exercise. To Jackie Barker for her encouragement and being there since the playgroup days. To Elaine Brydon for providing inspiration.

To Gordon and Suzanne for all their love and support.

To my sister Fiona for reading, listening and generally being the best sister I could have.

To my children David, Kate and Rachel. You are truly amazing and I am so lucky and proud to be your mum.

And to Martin, you are my everything and none of this would be possible without you.

ONE PLACE. MANY STORIES

Bold, innovative and
empowering publishing.

FOLLOW US ON:

@HQStories